The item should be returned or renewed by the last date stamped below.

Dylid dychwelyd neu adnewyddu'r eitem erbyn y dyddiad olaf sydd wedi'i stampio isod.

Newport
CITY COUNCIL
CYNGOR DINAS
Casnewydd

B4U 29/08/2019 .
24/7

To renew visit / Adnewyddwch ar
www.newport.gov.uk/libraries

INTENSITY

SHERRILYN KENYON

ATOM

ATOM

First published in the US in 2017 by Nemesis Publications
First published in Great Britain in 2017 by Atom

1 3 5 7 9 10 8 6 4 2

Copyright © 2017 by Sherrilyn Kenyon

The moral right of the author has been asserted.

A CIP catalogue record for this book
is available from the British Library.

ISBN 978-0-349-40666-4

Typeset in Caslon by M Rules
Printed and bound by CPI Group (UK) Ltd, Croydon, CR0 4YY

Papers used by Atom are from well-managed forests
and other responsible sources.

Atom
An imprint of
Little, Brown Book Group
Carmelite House
50 Victoria Embankment
London EC4Y 0DZ

An Hachette UK Company
www.hachette.co.uk

www.atombooks.co.uk

THE MEANING
OF TIME

W hen the world was new and time was young, there were no guardians for the gates. In the beginning, there was no need. Being fluid and flexible, time for many creatures wasn't a linear experience at all. Rather sentient beings moved forward and back at their whims and leisure. They could be born in the future and yet die in the past.

To them, the ability to move back and forth,

forward and back, was the same as breathing. They thought nothing of it.

For mankind who was born without such privilege, the concept was always a hard one to grasp.

To those who can bend time, the idea of a rigid linear lifetime without such freedom was just as inconceivable. These creatures didn't understand man's obsession with measuring and preserving what to them was an infinity of interwoven circles that bent back upon themselves with fluid ease.

But as with all things, abusers were born. Rather than being grateful for the abilities they had, they chose to prey on those who lacked them. They stole time from those who could least afford to lose it and used it as currency. Held it over the heads of those who needed it.

More than that, the abusers shifted history for their own gain, and created paradoxes and changes that ill-affected the entire world.

The entire universe.

It impacted everyone.

Even the gods.

The ancient writers claimed the original zeitjäger was born, not of a mother, but from just such calculated cruelty. When a demon abused time to hunt and kill his first victim for purely selfish reasons. That blood spilled in the name of hatred and violence hit the innocent ground of mother earth and mixed with her fertile soil to create a blood-red mud that made that firstborn golem. With no other emotion to nurture it than such malignancy, the golem became an insatiable nightmare that preyed on anything with a beating heart.

It became a conscienceless monster with an insatiable hunger for blood and bone.

Until the gods stepped in and gave the monster a soul. Worse, they gave masters to those monsters and assigned them a purpose. Enslaved them for their own needs, and made time a linear requirement for almost all creatures, everywhere.

One with rules and laws.

One with dire consequences for any who dared to tamper with its new rigid sequence.

Now tampering with it was something that not even the gods could do with impunity.

Tread not with time, for it slays us all in its own due course . . .

PROLOGUE

The end will begin. It always does. On the wind and with stinging pain. Faster than you can see and always when least expected. *Enemies will come and they will go—forever seeking to bring you low. But stand you must, and in even fewer trust. Thyself alone, thy heart of stone. One faith. One truth.*

One war.

And so it was long ago, and centuries in our future. One Malachai son who began his race. Whose true love and devotion to his precious Rubati caused them all to be cursed forever. So it began.

So it will end.

One Malachai son cursed to destroy the world because of the love of one woman. Or to save it because through her faithful heart he learned of salvation and forgiveness.

His choice.

To defy his destiny.

Or embrace his fate.

To build or destroy. The same decision that all humanity faces from the moment of birth. A road wide open to all that narrows with every decision made until we make the final one that ends our days with the last exhale we take to extinguish the candle on our lives forevermore.

Pawn or master. Choose wisely or perish from the foolishness of that last poor decision.

The immovable rock or the unstoppable force.

In truth, we are both. Situations have dictated and will dictate which we must be in order to survive. Today we are bitten, yet yesterday, we bit someone else. Tomorrow has yet to tell us which role will be ours, for it is in flux and could fall to either side.

Biter or bitten.

Life is ever a complicated symphony of catastrophes. Ever seeking to lay us low and lift us higher.

And no one has ever understood this better than the Ambrose Malachai. Born Nicholas Ambrosius Aloysius Gautier. Many things to many people. Son. Friend. Boyfriend. Squire. Brother. Dark-Hunter. Malachai. Demon. Husband. Father.

Betrayer.

Destroyer of the world.

Our could-be savior.

Nick stared at the stark words that condemned him. As harsh as they were, they were made twice as bad by the fact that they'd been written in his own handwriting.

In blood.

And they struck him like a blow.

With this he couldn't argue. His clairvoyance was flawless as he stood beside himself in the future, looking down at the words he was writing in his grimoire.

"How did I get here?" he whispered.

He still didn't know.

Because the future isn't set in stone.

His best friend Acheron's voice teased him from deep inside his mind. Every decision made impacted the next. An endless rippling stream of indecision.

One moment he'd been a clueless kid in high school. The next, he'd been a willing servant Squire for the Dark-Hunter Kyrian of Thrace. One who'd helped shield the immortal warrior from humans while Kyrian protected them from the demons who preyed on their lives and souls.

The next thing Nick had known, he'd become a Dark-Hunter himself. Only to learn that Menyara, his voodoo godmother who he trusted implicitly, was actually an ancient goddess who'd bound his own powers and hidden him from his demonic father and others who would kill or use him. That his true destiny was to become the demon who ate the world whole.

That had been his first lifetime.

Until he came back and tampered with it.

Or did he?

Man, Nick could lose his mind with this. Because what Ambrose—his future self—had failed to tell him was the secret he'd learned last night.

The secret he now knew.

For the first time ever, he understood Tabitha Devereaux's tattoo from his vision of their future fight, and why she'd placed it on her arm.

Not as a motto for herself.

A note to him to serve as a reminder . . .

Fabra est sui quaeque fati. She creates her own destiny.

That was why the Ambrose Malachai had stopped in the middle of battle to stare down at it. Why he'd screamed out in agony on the day he killed her.

I made myself the monster.

My choice.

Son. Friend. Boyfriend. Squire. Brother. Dark-Hunter. Malachai. Demon. Husband. Father.

Betrayer.

Destroyer of the world.

Or savior . . .

My choice alone.

As with all things. The future would be made by

the very decisions he made today. Good, bad and indifferent. He was the master spinner of destiny.

And he, alone, would bear it out.

"He will kill you."

Cyprian Malachai paused as those dire words hung in the air. A slow insidious smile spread across his face as he looked up from his homework to see the obsequious demon servant who stood on his left. "You don't know my father at all, do you?"

The demon stepped back into the shadows, cringing if the truth were known. Not that he blamed the creature. It was always good to fear him as he valued nothing and no one. That was the curse of the Malachai bloodline that he'd inherited from Ambrose.

They loved nothing and no one.

Except for his father. Ambrose had been cut from a different Malachai cloth.

Nicholas Ambrosius Aloysius Gautier. The so-called

Ambrose Malachai had been a unique creature unto himself. Out of all the Malachai born after their downfall and curse, he'd been the only one to ever know a mother's love.

The only one to have a family and . . .

Friends.

Something that baffled Cyprian to this day as no one had ever liked him.

He'd never understood his father's life or the loyalty of all those who'd died by Ambrose's side when they'd faced off in final battle all those centuries in the future.

Even now, he could see them as that fateful day had dawned. Lined up for battle. Both sides stood ready at the head of their armies. Cyprian's dark Mavromino forces had salivated for his father's *good*, Kalosum blood.

The Ambrose Malachai had stood strong at the front with his wife and her brother at his side. For the first time in all of history, the Naṣāru and Arelim had ridden to fight with a Malachai and his generals at their head.

As had the last Sephiroth. Brothers and sisters in arms.

All the forces of good and light had aligned themselves against Cyprian's demonic army. The primal sources of evil and night-shadow were ready and more than willing to finally take them all to their graves.

"Remember," Cyprian's mother had whispered in his ear as she prepared herself for war, "your father isn't as strong as he appears. Your mere presence here weakens him with every breath you draw while it strengthens you so that you can defeat him. Not to mention, half his army still thinks that he's betrayed them. It will take nothing for them to turn against him now."

Because they had no idea that Cyprian had been born. Or that he and his mother had been playing havoc with all of their lives by masquerading as his father. He'd been having quite the time playing Ambrose at all their expenses. None of the poor fools had been the wiser.

Not even his father.

Unable to tell the two of them apart, the sheep

had followed after him and done his bidding. They'd been duped without knowing. He made fools of them all, and he'd laughed at them the entire time.

Because they didn't know better.

For all his powers, the Ambrose Malachai wasn't impervious to everything. He had a great blind spot whenever it came to those he trusted and called friend and family. And Cyprian's mother was an ancient goddess of supreme power and vengeance. She'd promised Cyprian long ago that this day of reckoning would come.

And here they were.

Here they were . . .

Facing off so that he could rise to power and his father could die by his hand and exact revenge for her.

That was the way of the Malachai curse. The father perished whenever the son came of age and killed his father to take his place.

Only one Malachai could live at a time.

Today Ambrose would die and Cyprian would rise.

Embrace your fate.

And Cyprian had gleefully seized it that day on the field when he'd killed Ambrose.

Now he was in the past to make sure that day in the future came.

One way or another. And there was nothing Nicholas Gautier could do to stop him.

CHAPTER 1

This was a stupid idea. But then stupid ideas were Nick Gautier's specialty. In fact, when God had been giving them out, Nick had gone back not only for seconds, but thirds and fourths. Probably fifths, too.

Just ask anyone.

They'd all agree.

Especially his mother and friends. And none more so than his girlfriend, who was currently staring at him as if he'd lost his last three remaining brain cells.

He probably had.

Not that they'd ever worked particularly well whenever Kody was around. What with her tight jeans that hugged a very nice posterior, and those soft shirts she fancied that drained every last bit of blood from his teenaged Cajun mind and left it quite unable to function at full capacity. So even if he'd been a NASA rocket scientist, he'd have been rendered a blubbering idiot around her anyway.

He took comfort with that knowledge. Little bit though it was.

"Oh, Nick! You can't be serious." Nekoda Kennedy crossed her arms over her ample chest and blinked those gorgeous green eyes at him as if to say—*Son, you're a flaming moron.*

Yeah, of course he was. And dang it anyway. How could she be so attractive while calling his meager intelligence into question?

Yet there was no getting around it.

He loved her. Every inch of that tanned, delectable caramel skin that tempted him a lot more than he ever wanted to admit. Every bit of those cupid's bow lips he could spend the rest of his life kissing. Provided his mama didn't catch him, that was. No boy needed a lecture *that* stern.

Not to mention all her soft, curly brown hair he always wanted to bury his face in . . .

No doubt about it. He would always be a fool where his Kody was concerned.

And he was willing to die to keep her safe. Whatever it took. Running into burning buildings. Dodging traffic and irate Madre phone calls. Even facing ticked off demons, and the Apocalypse, with nothing more than his meager wits as weapons.

"I've got to do this, *cher*. It's a moral imperative."

"It's a grand stupidity!"

He touched her chin and grinned roguishly. "Nah! It's a matter of honor."

Rolling her eyes, she let out a long-suffering sigh that probably had to do with the fact that she'd been hanging with him all afternoon without a break— he couldn't blame her there as a lot of people made that exasperated sound around him whenever they spent this much time in his presence. Especially his maternal unit and his ancient Greek boss, Kyrian Hunter.

And no one more so than the Dark-Hunter Acheron, and Nick's demon bodyguard, Caleb. They both swore he could test the patience of Job and Ghandi.

Kody growled at him. "Fine. Go on and do it, you stubborn Cajun beast. Not like anyone can ever talk you out of anything so stupid once you've set your mind to it, anyway. But when you get a bellyache, I don't want to hear it. So don't come crying to me for Pepto Bismol later. I don't care how cute and sexy you are. I will not allow you to wear me down for *any* sympathy this time. Not over something you know better than to do. You can just suffer in silence. Alone." She stepped aside, clearing the way for him. "If you really think you can out-eat a Charonte demon . . . go for it."

Nick tsked as he stepped around her to slide into the empty folding chair, and inclined his head to Simi who was already waiting with a dozen plates of beignets for each of them. "Oh, I'm ready. You ready, Ms. Simi?"

Decked out in her black leather corset and purple ruffled skirt, the Goth demon grinned. "I's born ready, half-demon boy! The Simi done gots her barbecue sauce dugged out and is rearing to go. Less do this!"

Nick adjusted a plate and a glass of milk. "A'ight! And dang be he who first cries halt! Enough! I plan to eat till I snap the button off my jeans and make it a deadly weapon!" He popped his knuckles in preparation.

Off to the side of their table, Kody continued to growl at both of them. It was quite the impressive noise.

"What's going on?" Caleb asked as he came up to stand behind Kody on the sidewalk that looked out toward Jackson Square from the Café Du Monde where Nick sat with Simi, who'd already jumped the gun and started chowing down.

Kody gestured at them. "They're actually having an eat-off. Can you believe this?"

Caleb laughed. "He's an idiot if he thinks for one yoctosecond he can compete against a Charonte."

"Don't I know?"

"And yet you're dating him? Good job, woman. Way to raise those expectations. Yesterday, or in your case, years in the future, you were a demigod warrior, saving mankind from the demonic hoard out to annihilate them. From that to baby Malachai sitter. You didn't just fall off your high-and-mighty pedestal, Highness, you hit the ground and splintered to pieces, like Humpty Dumpty."

"Yeah . . . thanks."

Caleb held his hands up. "Hey, I don't judge. I fell just as far. Besides, I found a woman willing to actually marry my cantankerous demonic hide. After that, I will question no one's intelligence for the man in their life. Ever. My Lil really got the short end of it all."

Nick swallowed his beignet whole before he glared at his demon bodyguard, who was also *supposed* to be his best friend. At least that was what Caleb claimed and how the theory went. Though on days like this, he definitely wondered.

At well over six feet, Caleb Malphas had hair as

dark as Simi's and skin the same color of caramel as Kody's.

Yet the one thing that irritated Nick about his running-mate—aside from Caleb's rather caustic and biting barbs he never kept to himself and that were usually directed at Nick—were those Hollywood good looks that always left Nick feeling extremely inadequate. 'Course that was just a front. While Caleb might appear tall, dark, handsome and composed, his natural state of being was as an orange-fleshed, fanged demon.

Yeah, he was a total freak when he didn't have his human disguise up.

"Don't you have something better to do like raze a village? Haunt a house? Torment the damned? And I don't mean *me*. This *is* New Orleans, you know? There's a lot more condemned folks here than just my little Cajun hide. Look around. I'm sure you can find a lot more worthy target for your venom. Surely?"

"Yeah, but it's so much more fun to scare a little boy who's afraid of clowns." Caleb flashed an evil grin at him.

Nick shifted indignantly as he knew exactly what Caleb was referring to and he didn't appreciate it in the least. "Hey now, that thing ain't no clown I'm afraid of . . . it's a Mardi Gras jester. Get your terms straight, old man. Your senility's showing again. Besides, it's evil and talks under the light of your magic. And you know it. So don't you be hassling me over a well-founded fear about Mr. Creepy and his little head on a stick. That thing's nasty and whoever put it in the middle of a tourist district where they got little kids walking by it all the time ought to be tied naked to a Mardi Gras float on a cold rainy day and left there to be mocked. Just saying. It's all kinds of wrong."

And it wasn't like Nick was the only person alive with coulrophobia. That fear was quite common and normal. Maybe not for a Malachai demon who could tear a clown apart, but still . . .

Nick hadn't known he was the Malachai until many years after he'd developed his coulro-jester-phobia . . . on a stick. By then, his fear had become second nature.

Caleb made a rude dismissive noise before he passed a snide stare to Kody. "You know he's still having nightmares about that night?"

At least Kody defended him. "*I'm* still having nightmares about that night. I don't fault him on that account. It was pretty gruesome."

Yeah, and his father, the baddest Malachai ever born, had died in that battle.

And *all* of them had been wounded. The night they'd faced the talking jester with the tiny head, and the demon krewe had been *that* terrifying.

"Thank you, sug!" Nick kissed the air in her direction before he picked up another beignet and shoved it in his mouth whole.

"But I can't watch this." She turned her back and shuddered. "I'm getting diabetes just being here."

"And losing respect for your boy by the heartbeat," Caleb added.

To Nick's immediate cry of, "Hey!" Kody still ignored them both.

And neither of that kept Caleb from his merciless

quest to have fun at Nick's expense. "You're a ghost," Caleb reminded her. "You can't get diabetes."

"So you say. I'm willing to debate it." She shivered again even though she couldn't see their contest any longer. "I can't watch this insanity. Simi? You got my boy covered?"

Simi doused another plate of beignets with barbecue sauce. "'Course I do, Akri-Kody. The Simi won't let no demons or nothing else et your demon-boy or hurt him on my watch. Promise. Cross my heart, with barbecue sauce on top."

"Thank you, Ms. Simi. I'll see you two later."

Nick licked at the sugar on his fingertips as he watched Kody head off in the direction of her house. He cut a meaningful stare toward Caleb. "Speaking of . . . aren't you afraid your house guests are going to set fire to something? Like the whole, entire planet? Now that all three of the evil Celts are together and alone without adult or any kind of responsible supervision . . ."

Caleb went pale. "Yeah, clowns don't scare me. An unsupervised war god, hellhound and banshee . . .

this could have nuclear-level meltdown repercussions. Only thing worse would have been to leave Bubba with them. See ya later."

Wiping his hands down the leg of his jeans, Nick tried not to be too obvious. But he couldn't help the intense way he stared after them both, making sure they were completely out of sight before he returned to Simi. He brushed his dark brown hair back from his eyes. "Okay, I think we're safe now."

Simi looked up with a slight pout which was made twice as adorable given that her mouth was covered in powdered sugar and barbecue sauce. He didn't know why, but that combined with her black and red cybergoth pigtails made her look more like a kid his age than a demon who was thousands of years old. And while her speech was unorthodox to most ears, it came from the fact that English wasn't her native or primary tongue.

Charonte was.

Unlike the Malachai who could speak all languages with ease, she sometimes had trouble navigating between the two languages—especially with subject-verb agreement, something that often caused her to ramble as she tried to make sense of words that baffled her with their similarities.

To her, many of them were superfluous and unnecessary, as in humans should be able to follow her meaning simply by the context. And if they couldn't . . . Well, to quote Simi, poo on you.

Not that Nick minded her random jumps in logic or sequence. While he might understand and speak all languages, he was most fluent in Gibberish most days anyway.

And, he should get special bonus points for speaking in rapidly fluent Stupidity. At least according to his mom, and most of his teachers. If there was a wrong thing to say at a wrong time, he had a Ph.D. in it.

Dr. Nick Dumb-butt. That was him.

"What?" Simi battered her eyelashes. "You meant we gotta go *now*?"

"They might come back if we don't."

"Well, poo to that!" Simi sighed heavily in her obvious disappointment. "And here the Simi was all happy with her eats. You a mean demon-boy to drag the Simi away mid feastery!"

"That's what they tell me." And it was what he was trying his best to avoid. That and ending the world as they knew it. He'd really like to die centuries from now without causing the world to go with him on his way through the Pearly Gates.

Nick winced as that cold reality slapped him hard for the ten millionth time. He missed the days when he'd looked forward to a normal future of routine college, wife, kids, nine-to-five job, and growing fat, old and complacent with the world around him. When he'd been ignorant of his true destiny and future role in the larger universe.

It sucked to know that you would one day be the end of all living things.

At least that was what Kody and Caleb had led him to believe, but now . . .

They didn't know anymore. It was why he needed Simi to take him to Olympus so that he could meet his half-brother, the sleep god, and ask Madoc about time-travel and consequences. Nick needed answers and he didn't want anyone to interfere with the real stupidity he was planning. Which was exactly what Caleb and Kody would do if they were here.

They'd stop him from being even more suicidal than he already was. Warn him to stay away from Madoc and tell him why the last thing he needed was to cross those lines.

But as Kody had noted, he didn't listen whenever he had his head set on something.

Simi tucked her barbecue sauce into her coffin-shaped purse, then wiped her mouth. "Okies. Whenever you's ready."

"I was born ready for being an idiot." Nick braced himself for their trip through the dimension portals that he hated so much.

Simi blinked her eyes and jerked her head like a bird.

He felt that cold familiar, weird fluttering in his stomach that he got any time he had to cross into other planes or dimensions. Faster than he was prepared for, kaleidoscope colors twisted and blended and then quickly sorted themselves out. It was the strangest head trip. Like throwing hot crayons into a blender and leaving the lid off—something Nick didn't advise anyone doing unless they really wanted their mother to disown them or ground them for the rest of their natural born lives.

It took him a second to get his bearings. Especially since this wasn't where he was expecting to end up.

Yeah, not by a longshot. Confused, he glanced around the green and dark orange room that was way out of context. Had they taken a wrong turn at the bright light on the left? Or was this something else?

He'd assumed all of Olympus would be similar to Artemis's Greek temple, where he'd met the goddess before. Big columns. Lots of white and gold. Delicate marble things everywhere that made him extremely nervous as he was forever banging into stuff and knocking it over. 'Cause he never knew where his limbs ended these days.

That it would have some frescos. Gaudy paint. Weird fauna and robed attendants who were way too happy, given the unpredictable natures of the beings they served. That it would at least have something remotely *Greek* to it.

Yet this place contained nothing close to that. This was much more organic and dark and red. Contemporary. More akin to a kurazukuri home. So much so, he half expected a Pokemon or Team Rocket to come flying out at any moment and run him over. Or some unexpected Yakuza attack.

Yeah . . . it definitely had a Japanese feel to it. Right down to the bright, hand-painted rice wallpaper and austere, futon furnishings. There was even an ornate orange and green kimono hung on the wall to his left, and an antique yoroi hitsu beside it.

Scowling in confusion, he turned toward the Charonte demon. "Um . . . Sim? Where exactly are we? Did you mean to bring me here?"

'Cause this was definitely not Kansas and he was feeling about as lost as Toto wandering off the Yellow Brick Road. He just hoped they weren't about to encounter some weird, ticked off wicked witch, or a herd of screeching flying monkeys dressed like funky blue bellhops.

Better yet, he hoped no one dropped a house on top of him. 'Cause that was the last thing he needed right about now. And it would definitely ruin his already screwed up day.

Although, Simi did have on black and white striped leggings ...

Maybe she had more to fear here than he did.

Simi adjusted the strap on her coffin-shaped purse. "Well, the Simi knows what you said you wanted to go and visits with them nasty Greek god people who are all so irritating, but then I gots to thinking what you really wanted to ask about and so I thoughts—"

"Simi? What are you doing here?" The deep, thunderous voice radiated through the room with so much preternatural energy that it almost tripped Nick's Malachai blood against his will. Indeed, it took everything he had to stop his wings from unfurling and exposing him in front of the stranger. Something that would be about as embarrassing as his teachers calling him to the board during inconvenient moments at school when he'd been ogling Kody instead of his chem or lit book.

The fact that his Malachai blood detected that ancient, invincible power and wanted to react to it, set the last of Nick's nerves on edge.

Which meant this guy was *old*.

More than that, he'd have to be some kind of strong warrior demon for Nick's body to have reacted like this.

The stranger could probably kick his butt without effort.

Forget a house falling on him—that might actually be a far more humane death, than this dude setting claws or fangs to him.

And there was no doubt that this beast could take him in a fight and make it seriously hurt. Standing eye-to-eye with him—which was no, pardon the pun, small feat, he was like a super ripped ninja with the kind of toned muscles that Kyrian, Caleb and Acheron sported. Complete with his long black hair tied back in a sleek, neat pony-tail.

And by the stern expression on that face nothing got past those sharp, intelligent almond-shaped eyes that seemed to see through him. Like the

Dark-Hunter Acheron, this stranger appeared young, yet the air between them sizzled with enough arcane power that it said this man had been around a whole lot longer.

Centuries upon centuries.

Upon centuries.

He might even be older than Acheron. Maybe even closer to Caleb's or Dagon's prehistoric age.

And that was disconcerting. Especially as the Malachai powers inside Nick saw him not in the black t-shirt and jeans he currently wore, but in keikō armor wielding a naginata in the midst of battle against a group of dramonk demons.

His skill in that fight was unnerving, but not nearly as much as the next image that quickly flashed through his mind.

This was one of a crap-your-pants-sideways level of terror. No longer dressed in armor, he wore the guise of a zeitjäger. The creepy, creepy ravenesque demons who were in charge of monitoring time and anyone who would abuse it.

More than that, Nick saw him pulling off the

bloodied plague doctor mask they all wore to expose his eyes with an all black sclera.

Yeah, that's just what I needed today . . .

To have another run-in with those beasts. The one he'd had awhile back had been enough for his life. Nick really didn't want another.

Ever.

Simi, however, appeared immune as always to the scary thing in front of them. In fact, she ran over and hugged him!

'Cause yeah, that was a normal thing for someone to do . . .

In nightmares only.

"Akri-Tashi! I gots someone for you to meet!"

Nick cringed at the thought. Honestly? He'd rather meet his mom three hours after curfew, reeking of alcohol and wearing her best shoes.

On a Sunday night.

After missing Mass.

A slow smile spread across the man's face as he returned Simi's exuberant hug. Neither friendly nor sinister, that smile managed to hover somewhere between those two things. "Nick, good to see you, little buddy. Wasn't expecting the Malachai to come waltzing into my house today."

Oh yeah, that wasn't the least bit unnerving.

Nick let out a sarcastic laugh. "Dude, do I know you?"

His smile turned a bit warmer, which was even scarier somehow. "Takeshi. We've met in your future. *Many* times."

O-kay ... Nick was even more uncomfortable. "That supposed to make sense to me?"

Simi laughed. "You wanted to travel through time ... Takeshi do it lots and lots. Sometimes he lives backwards even. Though he not supposed to," she whispered. "So we not tell people about that ... shhh."

Ah, that explained it.

Sort of.

Yeah ... no. Nick was completely lost and confused.

Cocking his head, Takeshi scowled. "So what have you screwed up now, kid?"

Nick pressed his hands to his temples as his head began to ache from trying to keep up and understand what was going on. "Okay, I'm really on the losing end here. 'Cause I'm not sure what you're asking. Or even where I am, or what's going on."

Screwing up for him was like an Olympic sport. He did it so much and so spectacularly that he didn't even think about it.

Sometimes, like now, he wasn't even aware that he'd done it. At least not until Kody or his mom stopped talking to him for a day or two, and "stink-eyed" him every time he got near them. And left him every bit as confounded as Takeshi did on what Nick could have done to piss off everybody.

With a real laugh, Takeshi shook his head. "I know you, boy. While I don't live my life in a straight line, you do. And we shouldn't be meeting like this. At least not *now*. So for you to be here means you've screwed something up. What have you done?"

"You see what I was talking about, babe?"

Nick choked at the last voice he'd expected to hear.

But it at least answered the most probing question that had been eluding him for weeks now—where one of his generals and protectors had vanished off to. "Nashira? What are you doing here?"

For that matter, how had she gotten to this dimension?

Why was he even surprised at this point?

His yōkai grimoire being literally manifested in front of them. With long white-blond hair that belied her own Japanese heritage, Nashira had vivid purple eyes that were set in a beautiful, elvish face—complete with pointed ears that peeked out from her snow-white hair. Graceful and lithe, she moved like the wind and usually spoke in riddles that gave Nick more questions than answers.

And a resounding migraine he was sure was a brain tumor the size of a bowling ball.

At least that had been true in the past. Today, however, she answered like a "normal" human and not some pestilence demon sent to make him crazy.

"I came to see my husband."

When she touched Takeshi on the shoulder and

his harsh gaze softened, Nick's jaw fell south without any effort on his part. "Pardon?"

Takeshi took her hand into his and kissed her knuckles. Then he pressed her hand to his cheek and held it there as if it were some sacred object. "It's true. And I'm told that I owe her presence here to you. For that alone, Malachai, I'm willing to give you a great deal of slack and latitude."

Nick turned his gaping stare toward Simi. "Did you know about this?"

"That Akri-Tashi married? Well, yeah. Don't everybody?"

Given that Nick didn't know Takeshi at all, no. But he knew better than to refute Simi as the demon didn't like that. So, instead, he turned back to them and tried not to gape.

Nashira smiled. "I was an oracle long before I met Takeshi."

Okay, he'd go with that. But it still left him with one burning question.

"So you really were a zeitjäger?"

The fact that Nick knew about that part of his past

didn't appear to surprise Takeshi. "An exceptionally long time ago I wore that garb and played that role. Yes."

That wasn't exactly how Nick had been told those time-sentinel things worked. Rather his understanding had been you were born as one of them and had to do it forever. Like being a Malachai. There was no choice.

No escape.

Which begged one majorly important question. "So how did you get out?"

"Made a pact with Zev Kotori."

Takeshi said that as if Nick should know exactly who and what he was talking about, but again he had no clue. Maybe he should have been playing closer attention to all those Grim lessons, after all, and not ignoring the ancient being who hated him. There had been a reason why his father had sent Grim to tutor him—other than as another form of creative abuse. "Who?"

"The god of Time who was in charge of us back in the day."

Ah ... but it still told Nick nothing as he'd never heard the name before. It wasn't exactly something they referenced in his manga or fighting games. And God forbid they ever covered something useful in school. "From the bitterness in that tone, I take it that he screwed you over somehow."

"No. His sister, Tiva did. She's the Untime to his Time. And unlike her brother, she can't stand to see anyone happy."

"As a chaos goddess, she's the one who cursed me into a book." Nashira's eyes glistened from unshed tears. "It was her way of keeping me away from my husband. For no reason other than she was a jealous harpy."

Man, that sucked. Nick couldn't imagine anything worse than to be banned from Kody.

Well, maybe being locked in Caleb's laundry room with three week old dirty football jockstraps.

In August.

Yeah, his eyes watered just thinking about it. However, he'd veered off topic again.

Not that it mattered as Takeshi was quick to bring

them back to it. "You, as a Malachai, never released Nashira before this. In any known timeline or universe. Yet now she's here." He sighed. "I knew when she showed up out of the blue that you'd changed something about the past, probably major, but didn't really want to investigate. I was too grateful to have her back, whatever the cause. Now that you're here, I have no choice, but to face the fact that you've veered off the highway. So back to what I said . . . what have you done, boy?"

Nick shrugged with a nonchalance he didn't feel. "Stopped a couple of apocalypses. Fought a butt-load of demons. And managed to stay alive, much to my daily and eternal surprise."

Takeshi laughed.

And when he did so, Nick scowled as his powers kicked in with some unexpected disclosures. "Itzal Tsuneo." The name was out before Nick could control his involuntary verbal diarrhea.

It had a most chilling effect on his host. Takeshi manifested a dagger and had it to his throat so fast that Nick had barely blinked. "I will not be enslaved to you, Malachai!" He growled those words between clenched teeth.

His eyes turned an unholy red.

Nick held his hands up in surrender. "Wasn't trying to. Seriously." He needed to be more careful in the future. Of all beings, he knew the difference between common names and those used to summon, bind and control demons.

Itzal Tsuneo was the one that could be used to summon and control Takeshi. Worse? It could be used to enslave him the same way Nick's father had once enslaved Caleb and Grim.

"I would *never* do that to anyone. Dude, really. Not into using people or demons."

Nashira placed her hand over Takeshi's and pulled the blade from Nick's throat. "He's telling the truth, Neo. Ambrose is not his father or any of the others. It's why he freed me when he didn't have to." She leaned forward to whisper loudly in his ear. "Kill him, husband, and you know what horror will grow to power in his stead."

"You are ever my wisdom, Shira." He dissolved the dagger, yet continued to glare at Nick.

Nick glanced over to Simi. She didn't appear to be the least bit concerned by Takeshi's violent outburst. So much for her protecting him.

Or she knew Takeshi really meant that he wasn't going to kill him.

Hoping for that, he let out a nervous breath. "Okay then. At least now we know your parents didn't really name you Bob."

Which was the English equivalent to Takeshi, not so much in meaning as just in the routineness of it.

Takeshi finally laughed. "You're not as stupid as you look."

"Nah, thankfully, right? And what can I say? I'm addicted to manga." Nick winked at him. "And since you're not gutting me, I'm here to understand what was broken and how. Most of all, I want to repair it."

No sooner did he finish speaking than the room around them lit up with transparent and elaborate charts and lists that hovered in mid air. It was a spectacular display like something in a science fiction movie, only much better done. And a lot brighter and more intricate.

"What is this?" Nick breathed in awe of it.

"The time line of your life."

Nick's jaw dropped yet again. It was like looking out onto a foreign galaxy. Or the inside of a computer. Some spots were brighter than others. Some were white. Some blue. Some red and others orange. All were punctuated by writing he couldn't read—which was never supposed to happen to him. As the Malachai, he should understand all languages and writing. "What do the different colors signify?"

"The orange ones are your pith points." Those were the virtually unchangeable events. Things that were for the most part set in stone, and that could only be moved with the most catastrophic consequences and Herculean efforts. "Blue are the ones that will forever change your core personality." Takeshi cut him a sarcastic grimace. "Believe me, you don't want to tamper with those . . . Red are the ones that define your character." Takeshi grinned. "Some of those, you might want to consider changing."

"Thanks."

He didn't comment on Nick's interjection. "White

is your original path. Yellow are breaks where you've veered from what your timeline once was."

Crap. There was a *lot* of yellow and yet while it veered away a bit, it always looped right back to its original course. Like a snapped rubber band. Kind of weird, really. 'Cause from what Nick could see, he hadn't really changed anything. It was what Ambrose had said. For everything he tried, it went right back to where it'd started.

Nothing ever really changed.

The lines stayed basically where they'd been. Time didn't want to be changed. It fought back with a vengeance.

Nick stepped closer to the lights. "How can you see all this?"

Simi tsked at him. "He a zeitjäger, silly demon-boy! They can always see time maps. It why the Simi brung'd you here! They's much better for this than them Greek godlings."

It was impressive. He'd give her that. Scary, but impressive.

Nick held his hand up to touch the timeline. His

hand passed painlessly through the twinkling lights the same way it would go through some laser light show. The moment he made contact, though, bright green sparks lit up from his hand, across his chart.

Takeshi sucked his breath in sharply.

"What? What'd I screw up now?" That was the typical answer whenever things went haywire around him.

His features pale, Takeshi shook his head. "All that green . . ."

"Yeah? What about it?"

Nashira turned as white as her hair. "Is that what I think it is?"

Takeshi swallowed hard. "Yes." He met Nick's gaze and the feral fear that was deep in his eyes made Nick step back from him. "The green is where someone's trying to throw your life out of alignment."

That didn't sound good at all. In fact, it was making his ulcer bleed—not that he had an ulcer, but at this rate, one might be developing.

And having babies.

Nick swallowed hard. "I thought that was the yellow."

"No, the yellow is where *you've* changed it with the decisions you've made. And as you can see, it didn't really alter anything. That green is someone else. Someone who shouldn't have the ability to change anything in your life. And, kid, they're shifting your future even as we speak."

CHAPTER 2

C yprian froze as a strange sensation went
up his spine.

"Is something amiss, my lord?"

He cut a stinging glare to his obsequious minion.
With greasy brown hair, and pock-marked skin, the
slug demon was repugnant enough. That nasal tone
only grated his nerves all the more. To the point, it
was all he could do not to rip its head off and feast
upon its organs. "Where's my mother?"

"In her war room."

He snorted at the pun given the fact that his mother was Laguerre ... an ancient battle-goddess who didn't so much as invent the art of war as she'd perfected it.

It was what she lived for. Blood. Mayhem. Utter and extreme violence. Those were her happy, go-to places.

Like him.

Reversing his course, Cyprian headed for the paneled study that held some of the deadliest artifacts in the known universe. Ancient artifacts that currently included his mother and her ex-husband, Grim.

Cyprian hesitated in the shadows of the doorway as the two of them poured over some matter with great intent. They were ever plotting against someone—many times for no other reason than they'd been given the wrong order at the local coffee shop.

Since his mother was a goddess, she didn't appear more than a few years older than his teenaged body. But her beautiful, young looks were definitely deceiving.

As were Grim's.

Much like Cyprian's mother's long languid movements that belied her quicksilver lethality. She'd deceived many fools to their graves with her slowness. They never realized just how swift she was to anger or stab.

Until it was too late.

Her dark hair fell to her waist in thick waves. It was a stark contrast to Grim's lighter shade and stocky, muscled body. Together, the two of them had once led armies over the ancient world, destroying everything and everyone they came into contact with.

Good times that.

And why not? They were ancient gods of War and Death—the original riders who'd brought those concepts to the world of man and demon. Turmoil and chaos were what they lived for and what they both sought with every breath they drew forth into their not-so-human bodies.

Some thought that only Death could defeat War.

But Cyprian would take odds on his mother winning any fight between the two of them. She was vicious that way. Not to mention, she cheated.

They paused mid conversation to stare at him.

"Is something wrong?" his mother asked, making no attempt to hide her annoyance over Cyprian's interruption. Which made sense, given that she could barely stand her son and had never glossed over that fact for anyone's benefit.

Especially not Cyprian's. Indeed, she'd gone out of her way to *toughen him up* with insults and degradations to ensure that his skin was thicker than any tank brigade on the planet. At the rate she'd set fire to his more tender feelings, he should have bought stock in flame retardant Kevlar.

"Do you not feel it, Mother?"

Laguerre hesitated before she punched at Grim. "He's right. We've been discovered."

Rubbing his arm where a bruise was no doubt forming from her blow, Grim shook his head. "Not possible. Besides, look again. It's just another nosy zeitjäger who's uncovered our most recent actions. Ignore him and he'll go away. Or we'll kill him if he pursues it. Either way, it's of no consequence to us. I wouldn't spend three seconds worrying over it."

"I'm not so sure about that." Cyprian's gut remained tight with his uncertainty. "What if this younger Ambrose has found another way back to challenge us?"

"So what if he has?" His mother gave him a tolerant, yet irritated smirk. "It would be centuries before your birth. He has no memory of you or his precious wife as neither of you has been born yet. And in our time he died in battle only minutes after he learned of your existence. So even if Ambrose returns here, there's nothing to warn Nick about the future he's trying to avoid—we've shielded it too carefully. None of them have a clear vision of what we have in store for them. Our magick is too strong. Not even his little Nekoda remembers it clearly, thanks to our allies. Everything is working as it needs to. Therefore, we don't have to fear his interference. He knows nothing of his real destiny or any of those that are truly important. Trust in me."

She said that, but the Ambrose Malachai had already screwed things up by coming to the past so unexpectedly and had forced *them* to venture here in order to repair the changes he'd wrought that had caused a fracture in their plans.

Altered the world where Cyprian had ruled as the grand demon overlord and fulfilled the Malachai prophecy that his father had forsaken. He couldn't allow his father to screw things up again. This was what he'd been bred for and it was what he wanted.

All he wanted.

He jerked his chin at the red sfora on the desk near his mother's hand. It'd been taken from the Atlantean god, Acheron, when they'd defeated him in the guise of Ambrose. With that orb, they had access to all destinies, as Acheron had been born the final fate of everything. "Have you looked at it lately?"

"At what?"

"To make sure everything is fine?"

She leaned back in the chair with a peeved glare. "You doubt me?"

Of course he did. The only thing he didn't doubt was the sensation in his gut. *That* was irrefutable.

She was not.

More than that, she was expendable.

So he decided to call her bluff. "Well, if you're so sure, can we not go home? Why are we still in this godforsaken time period if all is right in the universe, as you say? Surely, we've spent enough time here?"

The light in her eyes went out as the smile faded. "Don't get cheeky with me, boy. I am your mother."

To whom he owed nothing as her maternal instincts amounted to the size of the head of a tiny pin.

Which made the Malachai in him rear up at her confrontation. "You need to remember who serves whom ... Mother. You may have given me life, but I allow you to live. And to serve at my leisure." He cut a glare to Grim. "Both of you. Therefore, I suggest you do as you're told and remember that though I might be in the skin of a teenager ..." He exploded into his real demonic body, complete with horns and wings. "It's only an illusion. I am the Malachai. Fully formed and unlike my worthless father, fully aware of who and what I am, and of all my abilities. And more than capable of destroying you both, even with your powers combined. Do not push me. Do not cross me. You are both my servants and *nothing* more."

Never one to be intimidated, his mother rose to her feet to glare at him while her breath came in sharp, brittle gasps. "And you'd best damn remember that even with all your magnificent abilities as you proclaim, a Malachai cannot travel through time without assistance." She raked a less than impressed stare over his body. "Even one who's fully formed. You have no other allies who will work with you by choice. Nor do you know anything more than your father's memories as they *were*." She glanced to Grim then sneered at Cyprian. "Like it or not, *boy*, you need us. So don't threaten me again, unless it's your wish to remain here and never reach the future you want to return to."

In that moment, it took everything he had not to choke her with his powers. To rip out her cold heart and feed it to the worthless snipe beside her.

But sadly, she was right. Every bit of it. For now, he needed her, whether he liked it or not. And he definitely didn't like this bitter taste of gall in his mouth.

His breathing labored, he turned on a hostile heel and stalked from the room. Yet with every click of his combat boot heels, he plotted their deaths in his mind.

And his father's.

"Your day is coming, Ambrose. The darkness dawns and I intend to ram it straight down your throat."

Again.

The memory of their battle to come was what he lived for. Especially after having been forced to endure in this primitive time period. Gah, it was amazing that mankind had survived as long as they had. Why they were so upset with his eradication was beyond him.

Honestly, he'd done them all a favor by wiping the human scum from the planet. They should have given him a medal.

Had they?

No. Instead, the thankless beasts had sent an Arel back in time to stop him.

Cyprian cocked his head as he heard his mother speaking with Grim.

"He's getting too big for his britches."

"Shh!" his mother snapped. "He'll hear you."

"It's ridiculous. We were riders of the Apocalypse. The chosen ušumgallu! You were the Šarru-Tahazu and I the Šarru-Namuš. Now ..."

"We will ride again. My father's almost dead. All we have to do is ensure the timeline remains as it should and return to our time period. Once Noir is weaker, we can take his blood and use it against Cyprian to bind him to us. Once we do that, we'll be the ones in control. Have patience, my love."

Cyprian felt the Malachai surging, wanting *their* blood. But as his mother said ...

Patience.

He'd come this far. He could make the distance. And if they thought to overthrow and enslave him as Noir had once done his grandfather, then they were about to learn the truth behind the Malachai.

Only one of his own blood could stop him.

That would be a son, which he didn't have.

Or his father . . .

"Not on my watch, old man." Just as that day in battle when he'd driven his sword through his father's heart and kicked him away to die, he would emerge victorious again.

It was the Malachai destiny to reign over this world. And while his father might be weakened by the kindness he'd learned from his Seraph mother, he was not.

Forget dancing in the rain. Before all was said and done, Cyprian intended to dance in the blood of every living creature.

And none more so than Ambrose Malachai.

Nick jumped as his phone rang. Stunned, he glanced to Takeshi, then to Simi and Nashira. "Um . . . anyone have *any* idea how there's a cell tower in this dimension?"

Takeshi snorted. "It's magick."

"Seriously, bruh? You took it there?"

He shrugged nonchalantly. "You asked. That's the

answer. I have to allow it for all the times Acheron comes to visit. Those Dark-Hunters of yours never leave that poor boy alone. I don't know how he stays sane."

Simi made a rude noise. "Ain't that the truthest? Ring. Ring. Ring. That ole phone ring so much, I swear The Simi hears it even in her sleep. I et it once and it made him real unhappy. Didn't make the Simi as happy as the Simi thought it would either. And no one wants to know what happens when it has to come back out 'cause them phones are not biologically degradeable."

Not wanting to think about that comment at all, Nick pulled his phone out. "Hey, Ma, sorry I'm—"

"Where are you, Boo?"

Nick winced at her hysterical tone. That was what his mom was most famous for. If he ever got out of her sight, she was like a bloodhound, tracking him down to the farthest reaches of the cosmos. He was surprised she hadn't tethered them together on his arrival from her womb, and insisted, rather than cut the cord, they find some way to fuse it together permanently so that he could never leave her side.

And while he hated to ever lie to her, telling her that he was in an alternate dimension with a couple of preternatural super beings was just a really bad idea. "I was feeling better, so I went out to grab a bite with friends. Didn't you see the note I left?"

Something strange was going on in the background. Were those sirens? He wasn't quite sure.

When his mom spoke again, it was in a low tone that sounded like she had her hand cupped over the mic. "Listen, baby. There's a situation here. Can you stay away for a while?"

What the heck? His mother *never* said things like that. At least not to him. All he ever heard was *Nick get your butt home. Now!*

He screwed his face up at the first thought that came to his mind. Especially since she'd gone to dinner with his mentor and best friend, Big Bubba Burdette.

Ah man, what had lunatic Bubba and Mark gotten her into now with their shenanigans? Those two could find trouble in a padded room, with both arms tied behind their backs.

His stomach sank to his feet as an even worse thought hit him.

"Ah, Ma! Please tell me you ain't doing nothing with Bubba. I swear to God, if I come home to a tie on the doorknob I'll be scarred for life. I am not ready to deal with the thought of that man as my new daddy."

"Oh my Lord, Nicholas Ambrosius Gautier! The things that you get in your head, boy! Don't make me hunt you down to spank you. Seriously! This has nothing to do with Bubba. Oh my Lord, boy! Really! *Really?!*"

"Then what?"

"The police just came here to arrest you!"

Nick froze as every bit of blood faded from his face. Bad flashbacks went through him from the last time he'd been wanted for something he hadn't done. "W-w-what?"

"You heard me! They're looking for a suspect to all the murders that've been going on."

Yeah, but why blame him? Only thing he was guilty of was hogging covers and sneaking french fries when Kody wasn't looking.

And one time only, he'd taken a sip of Xev's beer by mistake 'cause he thought it was Ginger Ale. Even that, he'd confessed promptly the following Saturday to Father Jeffrey and had done every one of his Acts of Contrition. And sworn to the Heavenly Father he'd never do it again until he turned twenty-one. Even then he wouldn't for fear his mom might not let him make it to twenty-two.

"What's that got to do with me, Ma?"

"Two of the victims were your friends, Alan and Tyree!"

Her words slammed into him like a physical blow. No . . . it couldn't be.

Nick staggered back into the wall. He wouldn't have been more stunned had she named Acheron, and Nick's Dark-Hunter boss, Kyrian, as victims. In fact, Alan and Tyree jumping him was what had led to him meeting Kyrian in the first place. When

Kyrian had saved his life after Alan had shot him on the street.

"Someone overheard you threatening to kill them, Nick. To get back at them for beating you that night. So the police want to question you about it. They think you wanted retaliation. You're their primary suspect."

"I didn't do it, Ma!"

"I know, baby. Kyrian and Acheron are talking to a lawyer about it, right now. But I didn't want the police picking you up and hauling you to jail without warning, like you're some kind of hoodlum. We're going to take you in, with their lawyer, so that you won't be booked and processed. I just need to know when you're coming home so that we can take care of this mess and not let you spend any time in jail!"

He was truly grateful for that. Last thing he wanted was to be locked up like his father. Especially now that he was a Malachai.

That kind of anger and viciousness fed his powers. Made him ruthless and stronger. Ate away his will and left him vulnerable to the bad side of his demonic tendencies. If left too long among those kinds of people, he might lose control and become a full blown demon . . .

Yeah, that was a terrifying thought.

And it was the last thing anyone needed.

Nick swallowed hard. "I'm with Simi."

"You're safe?"

"Definitely. There's no way the police can get to me here."

"Okay. Stay there and I'll call and tell you where to meet us so that we can handle this."

Nick hung up the phone and shook his head as he tried to make sense of the insanity. But that wasn't possible.

Alan and Tyree were dead. How? While it was true they'd been known to run with a rough crowd and get into things they shouldn't, it was still a shock to him. They'd once been inseparable brothers who had each other's backs, through thick and thin.

Dang . . .

"You okay?"

He blinked at Takeshi's question. "Can you show

me my friends on that timeline? Did Alan and Tyree die like this originally?"

"What do you mean?"

"My friends who shot me. Did they die in the first go round, before the timeline was tampered with?" He moved back to the lights and tried to read his roadmap. "I have to know what happened to them before Ambrose came back and started changing things."

Takeshi took him over to the first weird split. "Well, you weren't shot in the first sequence. You were stabbed."

"Why would that change?"

Nashira moved forward. "Because one of the possibilities in the new timeline is that you could go to prison for murder in retaliation for being shot and then mugged by them."

Takeshi nodded. "She's right." He pointed out the lines that intersected. "See how things build on each other. That's cause and effect. As you change something, it goes into a different direction and splinters off. This is now a new possibility that wasn't here before."

Nick was slowly beginning to understand. "Like in the Eye of Ananke."

Takeshi stared at him. "What do you know of that?"

"I had it. Caleb took it from me like an irate parent, slapped my hand, and told me not to touch it again or he'd slap my face next time."

"Good! You don't need to play with that. It'll only mess you up."

And boy had it. His head hadn't been right since. Though to hear most tell it, his head had never been right.

Some days, he agreed.

More green began to flash. "What's going on now?"

Takeshi laughed nervously. "Honestly? I'm not sure you want me to answer."

That didn't help his would-be ulcer any. "Ambrose told me to use the Eye to reset what I'd done. To go back to the beginning and not mess up anything else."

"Yeah, but you're not listening, Nick. It's not

what *you* did. Someone else is tampering with your timeline. This isn't about what *you're* doing. It's what they're *un*doing."

"Dude, you're seriously freaking me out."

"You need to be freaked out. This is bad. Everything is unraveling and you're walking a tightrope."

"Not helping!" Nick's only saving grace was that Kody wasn't here to hear the unmasculine whine in his voice. That was the last thing he wanted.

Or worse, for Caleb to hear it.

"You're misreading this."

They both turned to stare at Nashira.

"Pardon?"

She stepped forward. "Look at it, Neo. Carefully." With a delicate grace, she moved her hands over the lines as if playing some kind of instrument. As she did so, the lights shimmered and danced, then cleared.

Takeshi gaped. "She's right."

"I'm lost again."

He shook his head. "No, Nick. You're found. Just close your eyes. Count to three. And open them."

"Yeah, right. I wasn't born yesterday! Last time I did that, I got sucker-punched." His past had given him severe trust issues. He didn't blindly close his eyes for anyone. Not even to make a wish on his birthday cake.

Simi tsked at him. "You can trust them, silly boy-demon! Just doos what he says!"

Not sure about that, Nick growled and forced himself to do it. But it made every hair on the back of his neck stand up in protest.

Trust was not in him. With or without the Malachai blood.

Sheez!

Yet the moment he began to relax, he started to understand what they'd been trying to tell him.

Gasping, he opened his eyes and shook his head.

"You are the Malachai."

For the first time, Nick got it. Completely. He saw the universe as it was and his real and true place in it.

More than that, he had a quickening of the breadth and depth of his true powers. They flowed and united. Not just his, but all of the Malachai who'd come before him.

He was Monakribos. Jeros. Evander and Veres . . .

Yarin. Eli. Xul. Elyon. Xarex. Utu . . .

Adarian.

Ambrose.

On and on. All united. From first to last, throughout time. He felt that connection.

More than that, he saw how it all began and felt the rage of the first betrayal that had led to their creation. The hunger for blood.

Throughout time, his species had been on a quest for vengeance.

Nothing soothed it.

Not until the day Nick had found his Kody.

"I don't understand," he whispered.

Yet no sooner had those words come out of his mouth than he saw himself long ago . . .

CHAPTER 3

"So you're the son of Braith."

Standing in the middle of an opulent marble hallway, Nick blinked at the rich, melodic voice so similar to Kody's, and yet the accent was very different. Even so, this woman shared the same bright green eyes that seared him with intelligent curiosity, and a smile that made every part of his body sizzle.

She was just as breathtakingly bold as she walked straight up to him and arched her brow in challenge. "Have you nothing to say to me?"

Not really. He was too amused by the woman who barely came up to his chin. Her white wings twitched.

Her spunk and sass warmed him on every level. "And you would be?"

"Rubati. I've come to join the goddess's guard, but they told me that there were no openings. Apparently, there are so many Malachai here in the city that we're being sent back home without even being tested for skill. Pity." Sighing, she turned to leave.

Before he could stop himself, he reached for her hand.

"And why's that?"

There was no missing the confident gleam in her eyes. "I'm one of the best fighters ever born."

He laughed.

Faster than he could react, she flipped him onto his back and had a knife at his throat.

Impressed, he stared up at her, knowing that, had she wanted to, she could have killed him. "You made your point."

"I know." She stepped away and sheathed her knife. Then she held her hand out for him so that she could help him to his feet.

Thinking to fool her, he tried to flip her in turn.

Even then she got the better of him and once again, he ended on the flat of his backside, staring up at the amused twinkle in her eyes.

Until he swept his feet out from under her.

With a shriek, she crashed down on top of him. Laughing once more, he rolled and pinned her beneath him. "Draw, is it?"

With an indignant hiss, she reluctantly ceded his victory. "That was an unfair attack!"

"Really? You dare accuse me, given what you just did?"

"A little. Aye."

More amused than he should be, he rolled off her and helped her up. "I'm still impressed. And perhaps we can find a place for you in the guard, after all. Regardless of what they told you. Would you like for me to speak to the commander on your behalf?"

Her hopeful expression did the strangest things to his gut. Honestly, he'd never seen anyone more beautiful, nor had she been boasting about her skills. She was an accomplished fighter. "Could you?"

"Sure. On one condition."

"What?"

"Have dinner with me?"

Nick let out a deep breath as he realized he was seeing how Monakribos and Rubati first met, and how they started their doomed relationship.

Monakribos was the original Malachai who'd founded his lineage before recorded history had begun. It had been Rubati's vicious murder at the hands of her drugged and deranged husband as decreed by treacherous gods that had led to Nick's curse and prophecy.

His forefather had sworn his vengeance against them all for what they'd taken from him. He'd vowed to see the entire world burn over it.

The heart and soul of her husband, Rubati had been the anchor who had kept the first Malachai sane and manageable. She alone had made him "human". Once she was gone, he'd lost all shred of humanity and caring.

It was her DNA that she shared with Kody's mother that allowed Kody to be Nick's anchor in the future. And it was why he was their one hope of thwarting the Malachai curse. Because Kody's mother had been created from Rubati's blood, she, alone, calmed him. All because her mother had been born out of the injustice of Rubati's murder.

The gods had wrongfully taken Rubati's life and so to balance it out, Bethany had been resurrected without a heart to provide justice to the universe.

That was the legacy of Kody's bloodline. Her family were all gods of justice and balance. Chthonians or demigods.

Protectors of man.

Meanwhile Nick's were the destroyers. They were hatred and all the darkness of the universe.

By reuniting their two bloodlines, Nick and Kody stood a chance at laying the hatred aside and allowing Nick to live out his lifetime not as a destroyer, but as a protector too.

Haven't you figured it out yet?

Nick gasped as he heard his father's voice in the aether around him.

"Adarian?"

Something slammed into his chest, knocking him down. It felt as if he'd been hit by a truck. With a gasp, he forced himself to his feet, and braced himself to take another hit as he realized this wasn't who and what he thought.

This was the other Malachai.

"Where are you?" he roared. "Face me, you coward!"

Light blinded him.

And out of the searing brightness came the red and black winged beast who haunted his nightmares. The one with red, glowing eyes that hated him most.

Not his father.

Ambrose Malachai. The monster *he* feared becoming.

Beautiful and ugly in that he would one day incinerate the world. Or at least allow it to fall.

Nick winced as he faced himself in the vast

nothingness that hovered between dimensions. "Why are you here?"

Ambrose tsked at him. "C'mon, kid. You're not this stupid. I mean, you are. But think about it for a minute." He lifted his clawed hands up. The black talons shot fire toward the sky as his black wings spread out. Those eyes telegraphed their hatred and malice.

"What are the inherent powers of our kind?"

Nick scowled at Ambrose's question. "Necromancy." Which had been one of his hardest things to master and he was still working on it. The ability to talk to the dead wasn't something he could do with any kind of ease.

Not to mention, it was rather creepy. And the dead tended to be crabby whenever he tried it. They had nasty attitudes about being disturbed. Kind of like his whenever his mom asked him to take out the trash.

Ambrose nodded in approval. "What else?"

The first one he'd mastered and the only one he'd been born with that Menyara hadn't been able to bind or restrict. "Perspicacity." That ability to see the heart and truth of those around him. Whether it was the fact that Acheron was really a god or to tell whenever someone was lying to him, a Malachai could always see the truth of all things. Who and what everything really was.

Nothing and no one ever got the better of a Malachai.

Ambrose inclined his head. "Go on."

"Teleportation." They could move through connected space in short bursts, but not through time. Handy, but irritating to master in that Nick had screwed it up a lot in the beginning and had embarrassed himself royally as he ended up in a few places he hadn't meant to.

Yeah, not some of his finer memories. Puberty was bad enough. Puberty combined with sporadic bursts of popping in and out of rooms and clothes . . .

Nightmare levels that drove even the bravest into therapy.

"Next?" Ambrose prompted.

"Silkspeech." Another of the easier powers to

master. The ability to sway the minds of the weak and influence thought. To make them do or think what you wanted. One of Nick's favorite powers, especially with his teachers, and very handy for saving him from detention at school. And getting him out of parking tickets.

Sadly, it didn't work with his stubborn mother, or girlfriend. And if he tried it on Caleb, that resulted in massive bruising both to his body and ego.

"You're halfway there, kid."

Nick went for another aggravating one that misfired more than it worked correctly. "Clairvoyance." Because the future wasn't set, that one could be seriously tricky. The ability to see an ever-changing future was like trying to jump onboard a moving train. You had to time it correctly and make sure you didn't misjudge your steps. Or miss seeing the blurry telephone pole that was about to take your head off if you failed to see it in time. It also required opening his senses to the aether he was in now. To be able to see, hear and experience a heightened realm and to leave his body behind so that he could see the entire universe.

It was frightening here. A part of him was always scared he wouldn't make it back to his body. That he'd get lost and be adrift forever. But once tapped, he could find anything. Hear anyone. See the past. Present or future. It was like time traveling in a way. You just had to be able to make sense of it and understand it.

And not get drowned or overwhelmed by it all—a very tricky thing to do.

"And?"

"Dude! Don't rush me," he bristled at Ambrose. If anyone knew how much he hated to be pushed, it was himself.

Ambrose gave him a peeved, droll stare.

Yeah, well, he deserved it.

Nick cleared his throat before he continued. "Telekinesis." Another one that had been relatively easy to master. At least when it involved his Malachai tools. They usually came whenever he called them. Other objects could be a little harder as they had a tendency to hit him in the head and other body parts he didn't want to think about.

Mostly because that tended to make him walk funny for a few.

"You're almost there."

His pocket heated up to remind him of his favorite one. It was where he kept his pendulum at all times as he was prone to lose things. "Divination and conjuring." Again, they could be tricky, but so long as he stayed focused, they weren't so bad. And though most people thought divination was the same as clairvoyance, it wasn't. Divination and conjuring relied on using objects or tools in order to read signs or learn about the higher senses. Those were an entirely different set of skills.

Ambrose nodded. "Almost there."

"Summoning." And he definitely wasn't fond of it as the ability to bring or summon any demon into his realm came without any effort whatsoever. All he needed was their correct name.

Sometimes not even that. It was one power Nick could do without as it'd gotten him into all kinds of trouble over the years. Not to mention, his current "pet" Zavid. Although the hellhound would be the first to protest that label, it was still apropos. Nick hadn't meant to bind Zavid to him as a servant, but again, as the Malachai, it was just a little too easy to do it.

Sadly, it was much harder to break.

"You forgot one. The most important one, too."

Nick froze as he ran back through them. "No, I didn't."

"Yeah, you did. Think about it for a minute." Then Ambrose ran over the list again. "There are ten powers. You named nine. Necromancy. Perspicacity. Teleportation. Silkspeech. Clairvoyance. Telekinesis. Divination and conjuring. And summoning … That's nine."

He was right. 'Course there was a reason why he'd forgotten the last one. It was one Nick didn't play around with because it was the one he screwed up with the most. And it was the one you really didn't want to screw up as it had some of the worst consequences, hence Vawn's predicament of being a guy trapped in the body of a girl. And it'd been the one that had caused his friend Madaug to be turned into a goat for a while. "Transformation."

"Yeah," Ambrose breathed. "Transformation."

Nick froze as he finally understood what his older incarnation was trying to tell him. "Cyprian isn't in his real body."

"No. It's why you can't recognize him or feel another Malachai around you."

Just like he didn't see the Dark-Hunter bow and arrow mark on Ambrose's face whenever he appeared to him or the Malachai marks. Because they hid those. A Malachai could appear as anyone or anything he chose to.

Like Simi, or any of the Charonte demons. They could have any body or appearance they wanted.

Young. Old.

Crap . . .

And with a Malachai here, Nick's powers would be weaker and weaker. His son would drain him until he was too weak to fight. "Why is he here? Do you know? I mean, if he kills me, he won't be born. Right?"

"You have never learned to ask the right questions, kid. Don't you get it?"

He faded into the abyss.

"Wait! Come back!"

Nick growled in frustration. "If you know the answer, why don't you tell me!" He hated whenever they did that crap with him. Why did they have to play these games? Why not spill the beans and let him make soup or toss it?

"I swear I'm getting a tumor from all this!" Nick sighed as he listened to the voices in the aether and tried to sort through the madness of it all. Millions of thoughts came at him simultaneously. A cacophony of complaints, needs and wants. No wonder the gods tuned them out. You had to or you'd lose your mind.

It was unrelenting. People ricocheted through life like random pinballs speeding through one giant machine. Everything about it made him dizzy.

Honestly, he didn't know how Acheron remained sane. In some ways, he wished Ambrose had never told him about his future.

Closing his eyes, Nick tapped the very powers he'd mentioned. His clairvoyance opened and left him standing over his mother's body.

Left him in the darkness of his own home, feeling betrayed by Acheron and Kyrian for allowing the Daimons they fought to murder her in cold blood.

More than that was the guilt. He should have been there. Tears streamed down his face as pain lacerated him. His mother had given him life. Had sheltered and protected him with everything she had. And how had he returned her love?

He'd left her defenseless when she needed him most. On the very night when the Daimons had come to his door in the guise of a Dark-Hunter, Nick had been out with the other Squires patrolling to protect strangers.

Not his mother.

He'd left her in the hands of the immortal protectors who'd sworn to keep humans safe from the demons who preyed on them. Trusted in Acheron and his army to shelter the only person he needed and loved.

A woman who had been kind and caring toward all of them. Nick choked on a sob as he saw her throat slashed open and her glazed, glassy eyes that accused him of carelessness.

This was his unstoppable future.

The one pith point he couldn't change. No matter what he tried, all roads led him here.

Throwing his head back, he shouted out in agony. Why couldn't he save her? With all the powers he had?

We are destruction . . .

The voice of the Malachai whispered through him. It was a thunderous, dark sound that he knew well. An amalgam of all his predecessors. Older than time, it reverberated through his entire being.

With it came that surge of power. Primal and raw. Nick forced it down. He didn't want to go Malachai.

Not now.

He needed to stay rational and to figure this out. He couldn't give in to the hatred. There was too much on the line. Too many that he cared about.

"I won't let you tell me who I am," he breathed. "I am Nick Gautier." Tomorrow, he might become Ambrose Malachai. But it wouldn't be today.

No. Not today.

Suddenly, his phone rang. Jumping, he answered it, no longer thinking it peculiar. Peculiar was becoming his new middle name.

However, that being said, what he did find shocking was to find Virgil Ward on the other end.

"You remember me, kid?"

"Um, yeah."

As a blood-sucking attorney, literally, Virgil was a hard creature to forget. A little over six feet tall, he didn't appear to be any older than sixteen or seventeen—Nick's age when Virgil had been turned into a real vampire after a demon had bitten him. Now he spent eternity working night court for the damned and preternatural as part of the Laurens and Ward Law Firm in a posh downtown office.

Virgil was also the only one whose powers of persuasion and masking put Nick's to shame. That boy could pull the wool over anyone's eyes.

"Good. I just got off the phone with your mom and I'm going to walk you into the police station to see about this matter where they want to talk to you, and make sure you don't hit lock-up, for reasons we all know. Where are you?"

"Do you know a guy named Takeshi?"

"As in the zeitjäger, kick-your-hide-sideways?"

"That'd be the one."

"Very familiar. Still have the boot prints on my left cheek. You with him?"

"Affirmative."

"Good lad. Safe place. I like it. Can you put him on the phone for me?"

Before Nick could answer, a strange buzzing started on the line. One that drowned out Virgil's voice. His vision dimmed. Pain exploded through his head and left him in absolute agony.

What the heck?

He blinked in an effort to clear his vision. Yet all it did was make him queasy. Dizzier. The darkness lifted into a bright, searing light that made it even harder for him to see.

Tires squealed.

Before Nick could recover, something slammed into him and sent him careening through the air.

An instant later, he landed on the pavement and realized that he'd been struck by a car.

Unable to move, he lay in the street as his entire body throbbed. Voices assaulted him. He tried to get up and focus.

Everything was hazy and surreal.

You are mine, Malachai. And I will make you bleed . . .

CHAPTER 4

Nick could feel the breath of his son on the back of his neck as his powers weakened and left him feeling drained and helpless. For the first time in his life, he understood his father's animosity toward him. It was an involuntary survival instinct built in to their Malachai DNA that wanted to destroy anything that threatened them.

It was innate and primal. Terrifying. The fact that his father had gone down protecting him and his mother said a lot for Adarian.

That alone allowed him to finally forgive his father for the sins that had created Nick. Allowed him to let go of the hatred and anger he'd borne for the creature who'd sired him. For the first time ever, he understood his father's mind set.

And what made his mother such an incredible gift. Even after all the horrors his father had put her through, she'd still been able to find the good in both of them. Rather than hate Nick for the violence of his conception, she'd found a way to see past the horror of it. Never once had she held his father's acts against him.

You are my most precious baby boy, Nicky-Boo. There's never anything you could do to make me not love you, through and through. For you are, and will always be, my baby angel.

It was why the thought of her future murder crippled him now and would one day destroy him. She truly saw no evil in this world.

For he was a Malachai born of equal part Mavromino and equal part Kalosum. Like the firstborn, Monakribos, Nick alone shared that unique birthright.

So how then, could he have a son born of such hatred that he could feel it crawling over his skin like a living creature? This amount of venom came straight from the Source. He sensed it as if it were a part of him.

All Malachai were conceived in violence to do violence and to die violently.

Yet Nick knew that he'd never, ever be able to harm another person that way. It just wasn't in him to act the way his father had.

Never. He knew himself better than that.

Laughter echoed in the aether, in and out and all around as he pushed himself to his feet. Something else sizzled.

He turned a circle in the darkness, seeking some hint of the malevolent child he could feel and not see. Why were they playing this cruel game of hide-and-seek?

Suddenly, he was surrounded. The very shadows emerged into the light to attack.

These were the kinds of demons he knew well.

With his Malachai powers, he summoned his

sword and went after them. He felt the familiar surge of rage, but quickly pushed it down. *Don't give in.* He knew better than to let his anger rule him. In spite of what Caleb and Xev thought, he was paying attention during his lessons.

He heard his instructors and friends.

Most days anyway.

He spun and caught the first demon behind him with a vicious blow that caused it to shrink back into the darkness. Another came forward to attack. Nick barely countered in time to keep it from slashing his arm. But he severed its hand. It shrieked and withdrew.

"Nick!"

That was Virgil's voice.

Nick's sight dimmed. Everything shook and spiraled. What he heck? He wasn't sure what happened. Not until he began to fall through the aether again.

What was this feeling? It was as if he had no grounding anywhere. Something was pulling him against his will. He had no control.

Not until he found himself back on the floor of

Takeshi's home with Simi, Takeshi and Nashira standing over him like a group of worried parents.

Blinking, he stared up at them. "Having that moment where I feel like my mom was calling me for dinner and I was on the last level of a videogame and didn't hear her 'cause the big boss was almost dead and there was no pause on the game."

Takeshi rolled his eyes. "Feeling like that parent who wants to beat my kid, but can't because I don't want to go to jail and ruin my credit scores."

Nick scowled. "Bruh, that makes no sense."

"Neither does what you just said. Now you know how we feel."

Snorting, he took Takeshi's hand and let him pull him to his feet. "What happened?"

"Don't know. Your eyes rolled back in your head and you hit the ground pretty hard. You okay?"

Nick rubbed at the large bruise that was forming on the base of his skull. "Major concussion would definitely explain the rodier I just went on."

"Rodier?"

"You know ... wander about aimlessly? Drag the

streets? Make a pass through … Never mind. I've gone Cajun and y'all looking at me like Kody did the first time I asked her if she was playing *rat de bois* with me or if she wanted to go make groceries."

Takeshi scowled. "Do what?"

Nashira shook her head. "*Rat de bois* means opossum. The other means he's going to the market for food."

"Seriously?"

She nodded. "Hanging out in his pocket has been quite the education."

"I can imagine."

Nick snorted. "Hey now, don't you even slap on me given the random acts of violence against the entire English language that comes out of the mouths of Aeron, Vawn and Kaziel. I only get about one-fifth of everything *they* say. Some days, not even that much."

Laughing, Takeshi brushed his thumb against his bottom lip. "So what happened?"

"I don't know. I got snatched into the aether by … something. The other Malachai, maybe? At least I think that's what happened." Nick pressed the heel of his hand against his eye to ease the ache there. "How can he be here? And who the heck is he? Who's his mother?"

Nashira and Takeshi passed a look between themselves that said they knew the answer, but had no intention of sharing it.

"C'mon, guys! Really? You can't sit on this one! You have to tell me something. Especially if you know who he is."

Takeshi shook his head. "Nick, you know the law and how this works. The more you know, the worse it gets."

"Then why do I have Clairvoyance at all?"

"Do you?"

He had a point and Nick hated him for it. From what he understood about the power, even when it worked, it wasn't foolproof. "Why do *you* have it?"

"Because I don't use or abuse the power. I know how dangerous it is to tamper with things best left undisturbed."

Nick was about to snark at him when he felt a

peculiar sensation go through him. One that was unmistakable and left him sick to his stomach.

Eyes wide, he met Simi's gaze. "Kody's under attack!"

Without waiting for anyone, he teleported to her house. To his horror, he found her there, surrounded by more than a dozen mortent demons. True to her breeding, she was holding her own. But she'd broken a good sweat and was definitely outnumbered.

"Need a little hand, *cher*?"

She passed him a disgruntled grimace. "Nah, sugar, I got this. Go have some lunch."

Laughing at her sarcasm, he manifested his Malachai sword and moved in to protect her back. Still the demons kept coming. It was like a bad dream.

"How are they getting in?"

Kody shook her head as she parried another assault. "No idea. I had everything locked down. Nothing should have been able to breach *my* shields."

Nick hissed as the demon he was fighting caught him with his fangs. Punching the wretched beast knocked him away. "Well, this isn't fun!"

Simi, Takeshi and Nashira finally joined them.

"Did y'all get lost?"

"No. Her sigils blocked us."

Kody lopped the head off the demon she was fighting before she gave him an I-told-you-so stare.

"Yeah, but they're here. You can't argue with *this*." He gestured at the carcasses of the smelly beasts lining Kody's floor.

"I know. It defies my best ability to explain it." Takeshi glanced to Simi who was staring at the wall. "What do you see, Sim?"

"The evil Arel. He did this."

Kody gasped. "Sroasha?"

Simi nodded. "Him mad that you not kill Akri-Nick. So he now working with them Grim and War to kill you, Akra-Kody."

"Well, that's a load!" Nick felt his eyes change as his powers surged from the rush of anger that went through him at the thought of Kody being harmed. Especially because of him. "I thought we'd gotten rid of those pricks."

But he knew better. That had been wishful thinking on his part. The Arelim controlled Kody. They were the whole reason she was here. The reason she'd been brought back from the dead in the future and sent back in time.

Her eyes sad, she cupped his face in her hands. "Breathe, Nick. It'll be fine."

He didn't believe it for a minute. Everything was spiraling out of control, faster than he could catch it. Faster than he could catch his breath.

She kissed his lips, then grimaced at him. "And why are you here with Takeshi and Nashira?"

"You know Takeshi?"

What a stupid question. Of course she knew him. She knew everyone.

"He was friends with my father and uncle."

Nick didn't miss the odd light in Takeshi's gaze as he studied Kody. "What's that look mean?"

"Déjà vu."

Now it was Nashira's turn to go pale. "You can't have that."

"Yeah, I know. But I'm having it anyway, and it's

freaking me out as much as it is you." Takeshi jerked his chin toward Kody. "The last time I saw her, she was a grown woman. She's not supposed to look like this. That's not her body . . ."

Kody scowled. "Pardon?"

Takeshi crossed his arms over his chest as he surveyed the house and the dead demons on the floor. "You don't remember your life, do you?"

"Of course! I remember my father and brothers. My mother . . ."

"What do you know of Nick?"

"He killed me and my family."

Takeshi let out a nervous breath. "No, Neria. He didn't."

She narrowed her eyes and stepped back in confusion. "Are you sure?"

"You know I would never lie to you. Have you really forgotten your children?"

Indecision played across her features as she shook her head. "I was a girl in battle."

"No, you weren't."

Kody glanced back at Nick and the uncertainty in

those green eyes scorched him. "It makes sense, in a weird way. I think that's why I couldn't kill you when I first met you like Sroasha wanted me to."

Takeshi gaped. "Pardon?"

She swallowed hard before she spoke again. "He sent me back in time to stop the Malachai. First Jeros and then we went through several of them. I failed each time because they were far more powerful than I was … until we got to Nick. Him, I could have taken. Easily, because he hadn't come into his powers yet. He was too young and ridiculous when I met him. But for some reason, I couldn't bring myself to take the killshot even though I knew he'd eventually go bad and kill everyone I loved. I kept seeing the good in him and thinking that he could be saved." She cupped Nick's cheek. "There was something about him I couldn't resist."

"It's the Rubati blood in you. Instinctively, it calls to Monakribos, regardless of the incarnation of your own body. And that's why Nick is leashed with you by his side. You anchor him, just as she anchored Kree all those centuries ago."

"But then why would Sroasha want me to kill Nick? Especially if he wasn't the one who destroys everything?"

Simi tsked at her. "Make total sense, Akra-Kody. 'Cause if the bad Malachai demon-boy had already kilt you and Akri-Nick, then he'd be stronger. So the best way to beats him would be to kills his father afore he's borned."

"She's right. It'd be the only way to stop him, especially if you don't know who he or his mother is."

Nick scratched his head. "I'm still so confused by that. If I'm in love with Kody and I know it, then I know I didn't two-time her with someone else. I'm not that kind of dirtbag." He jumped as his phone rang and startled him. "Sheez!" Grabbing it, he saw it was Virgil again. Sheepishly, he answered it.

"Where are you?"

"Sorry. Had a little demon trouble to take care of. We're on our way. Be there in a few." He hung up. "I have to meet Virgil and go to the police station."

Kody's eyes widened. "What?"

"Yeah. It's good to be me." He sighed. "Let me get this over with and then we can clean this mess up."

"I'll tell Caleb to meet you there. Just in case you get stuck."

He started to tell her not to be so paranoid, but they were talking about *him*. Yeah, with his luck, a backup plan was always a smart idea. Things tended to go sideways as soon as he lifted his head off the pillow. Sometimes before he even opened his eyes in the morning.

Sliding the phone into his pocket, he faced Takeshi. "Anything I need to know going into this?"

A deep, dark red light flickered in his eyes. "The future is determined by the decisions you make every second of the day. Victor and victim. Both come from the Latin word, *victus*. To vanquish or be vanquished, yet the original meaning of victim was to be a living entity killed and offered in sacrifice to some higher, supernatural power."

Those words sent chills over Nick. "Invictus." It

was the tattoo on Ambrose's arm that meant *uncon-
querable. Never subdued.*

Like his friends Bubba and Mark always said, you
might kill me, but I'll be taking you to hell with me
so that I can chain you to the throne of Satan myself
and spend the rest of eternity whupping your ass.
That was the Southern way.

It was also very Cajun and vintage Malachai.

"No dang demon kills me and lives. On that you
can bank." Nick held his hand out to Takeshi.

Takeshi smiled as he shook it. "That's the Ambrose
I know. Take care. I'll be seeing you, kid." He vanished and left Nashira.

Kody frowned. "Caleb isn't answering his phone."
She hung up. "Can you reach him?"

Nick didn't bother with the phone. He used his
powers to call out for his surly bodyguard. "Yo! Baby
Cay-Cay? I'm doing something stupid and dangerous. You gonna come knock me in the head for it?
Or do you plan to let Simi have all the fun honors?"

Caleb didn't answer.

An awful feeling went through him.

Where was Caleb?

Kody swallowed hard. "He's not answering you either, is he?"

He shook his head. "I can't go to Virgil until I make sure Caleb's okay."

"I know. We'll meet you there."

They all teleported to Caleb's front door. Nick would have gone inside since he had permission to get past Caleb's sigils, but he wasn't about to pop in alone when he didn't know what was on the other side, waiting to devour him. While he was about as reckless as anyone could get he wasn't particularly stupid as that tended to be fatal in large doses.

So he paused until Simi, Nashira and Nekoda caught up to him. Then he knocked on the door of Caleb's huge antebellum mansion. The sound echoed through the place.

No one came to the door.

Nick passed a grim stare to the women. "All right. I'm going in first. Simi, anything rears its head, barbecue it up."

Rubbing her hands together, she smiled so wide it

showed off her fangs. "Oh goody! The Simi knews there was a reason she loved her demon-boy!"

Not wanting to think about that, Nick took the knob in his hand and used his powers to unlock it. He opened it slowly, expecting snot-demons, hell-monkeys ... who knew what to come flying at him.

But there was nothing in the foyer. Dark and quiet, the house seemed abandoned.

"Caleb? Vawn? Aeron? Xev? Anyone? Bueller? Bueller?"

Snorting at his joke, Nashira jerked her chin toward the staircase. "Upstairs. I heard a groan."

Nick bolted for the steps and took them two at a time. He didn't slow until he reached Caleb's upstairs study where he found them wounded and bleeding. "Oh my God!"

In his orange demon form, Caleb was flat on his back and lying with a blood-soaked cloth over his abdomen. "Not exactly the right entity." Then, he groaned.

Aeron grimaced. "Be speaking for yourself, demon. When I lay me hands on the bloody knackers, I'll be teaching them what it is to come at a war god unawares. Ain't been hurt like this since the time I ran afoul of The Dagda."

Vawn nodded in agreement as he drew a ragged breath. "They came upon us like a pack of jackals. So fast we ne'er saw them until they had us all bleeding."

"Who were they?" Nick knelt beside Caleb while Kody checked on Aeron.

"Sephirii."

Nick froze at the last word he expected out of Caleb's mouth. "Pardon?"

Kody shook her head. "That's impossible. They were all put down."

Caleb pushed himself slowly to his feet to face her. His features were strained and earnest while he held his makeshift bandage against his ribs. "Yeah, I know. I was there. I saw them fall. But I also led my army against and for them for hundreds of years. Believe me, I know a Sephiroth sword when it cuts me." He pulled the cloth away to show them the grisly wound on his stomach. "Nothing else looks like this, cuts as deep or burns half as much."

Nick screwed his face up at the painful sight. "Bruh! There's ladies present. Cover that!"

Kody ignored his outburst. "Jared is the only Sephiroth left and he's imprisoned. His sword was destroyed when they enslaved him."

"Yeah, I heard that lie, too." Caleb pointed back at his wound. Then he threw his head back and let out a shout that practically shook his rafters. "Shadow! Get your rank, worthless carcass here. Now! Don't you dare drag your ass or I'll kick it every step from here to Avalon and back."

"Sheez almighty, demon. What's your dama—" the disembodied voice broke off as a man materialized in front of them and he saw Caleb's wounds. "Oh . . . you really are damaged."

About half a foot shorter than Nick, he appeared to be mid twenties, with hazel gray-blue eyes that held a storm inside them. The man's hair was a strange shade. Neither light nor dark, it held strands of both and managed to fall between the two colors. And he wore it pulled back into a short, tight ponytail. The one good thing about him was that unlike

Aeron, Kaziel and Vawn, his British accent was light, pleasant and easy to understand.

Caleb glared at the man as if he could rip his throat out. And the funny thing was, he didn't react to Caleb's venom at all. He was so cool about it, he practically bled icicles.

"So Shadow, explain to me how it is we were just attacked with Sephirii swords."

Shadow blinked twice before he glanced around at each of them. Still so nonchalant that Nick admired his ability to show nothing. Dang, to have that amount of control over his emotions. He'd never get in to trouble for anything. "No idea."

"Really?"

"Really."

"So, you're telling me that you really destroyed every last one of them like you were instructed to do after the Primus Bellum?"

Only then did his facade crack. In fact, his expression was the same one Nick got whenever his mom asked if he was the one who'd forgotten to put the toilet seat down. Which she already knew the answer to since he was technically the only guy in the house—and Xev didn't count because he was in the disguise of a cat and his mom didn't know it. And well, the nasty buggar never forgot to put it down once he was finished. All that aside, Nick hated it whenever she pulled that crap with him, as it was grossly unfair. Although, to be honest, he'd tried to blame it on space aliens a couple of times.

And that had gone over about as well as Shadow's next words. "Basically. I destroyed the vast majority of them. Yeah."

Aeron cursed, then started for him, but Vawn caught him and held him back.

"Define *majority*," Caleb said in a voice that let it be known Caleb was only one wrong syllable from unleashing Aeron all over Shadow.

"I was given counter instructions by someone I trusted."

"Who?"

Shadow shook his head. "I took a vow to never disclose that. But I believe what they told me."

Caleb let out a feral growl. "You're an idiot."

"Of course I am. I followed you into battle, didn't I, *Commander*? And what did it get me?"

A tic started in Caleb's jaw. "As I recall, you came out of it a lot better off than I did."

Shadow took a step forward and lowered his voice to that demonic, evil tone. "You really want to compare those scars, Malphas?"

Nick stepped between them. "All right. Ding! Ding! Fighters to your corners!" He gently nudged more room between them, then turned toward Shadow. "If you think the swords are where you left them, check and see. It's an easy fix. Let's make everybody happy. How 'bout that?" He met Caleb's gaze. "Would that satisfy you?"

Stepping around Nick, Caleb slugged Shadow.

Shadow took the blow without flinching. All he did was wipe the blood away with the back of his hand while he glared angrily at Caleb. "Calm down. I took them into the Nithing. Nothing can get to them there."

"Something did! I was just attacked by a group of them, including Takara!"

Shadow went pale. "Impossible."

"If one more person says that word to me today I swear I'll gut them!" Caleb growled those words out between clenched teeth. "I know my brother's sword."

Technically, it was his nephew's. But since no one was supposed to know Xev was Jared's real father, Nick didn't bother to correct Caleb. Obviously, he didn't trust Shadow with their well-kept secret.

Shadow stepped back. "No one, and I mean *no one*, knows that I have those swords."

"Are you sure?"

He nodded. "Not even Jared was told."

"How did you end up with them?" Nick asked.

Shadow let out a bitter, scoffing laugh as he raked him with a look that said he equated Nick to a talking gnat. "Who are you and why are you bothering us?"

Nick curled his lip as he let his own offense show. "Not the goo on the bottom of your shoe. That's for sure."

Caleb rolled his eyes. "He's the Malachai."

"*Him?*" He burst out laughing, until he realized Caleb was serious. "Really?"

"Yeah. Don't underestimate him."

The pained noise Shadow made said he was doubting, big time. But then, Nick was used to that.

Clearing his throat, he returned to Caleb's question. "I hid them deep and have never breathed a word about their location. I knew better."

"What about Lombrey?"

"Not even he could have found them. Believe me."

"Yeah, well. Somebody did, Shadow. I didn't stab myself." He gestured to Vawn and Aeron. "And you're lucky I'm not feeding you to *them*. Especially given how ticked off they are right now."

"You're sure it wasn't a Sarim medallion sword you faced?"

"I know the difference. Like Nick said, go and check if you doubt me."

"Fine! Let's go! This I can prove." He held his fingers up and snapped them the way someone would irately summon a waiter. An action that would most likely end with water being "accidentally" dumped on their head.

The moment Shadow did that, a whirlwind whipped through Caleb's elegant home.

Nick instinctively reached for Kody.

Simi grinned. "Can the Simi eats the Fringe-Hunters if they comes near us, Akri-Shadow?"

"Only if they attack you, Sim. And if they do, please, have at it."

When the winds cleared and Nick could see again, they were in a strange surreal place. Neither light nor dark, it was a shadowy realm that reminded him of Azmodea where the hellchaser, Thorn, made his home, except everything here was an eerie gray. There was no color whatsoever. "Where are we?"

"The Nithing. It's the shadowland between realms. Like perpetual dusk."

"It's creepy."

Shadow didn't say anything in response to that as he led them to a peculiar looking forest of gray twisted trees. Trees that had almost human-like features.

"You hid the swords in the forest of Woe?" Caleb gaped.

"Last place anyone would look."

"Yeah, you're right about that."

Nick wasn't sure what that or Caleb's irritable tone meant. "Why?"

Kody snorted. "It drains their power and that of any and everything that comes here. Actually, it's a great place since that would keep them about as hidden as being destroyed."

Shadow touched his nose in approval as he nodded. "Exactly. Out of the hands of all evil beasts."

"Except for you?"

He glared at Caleb. "You went there, Mal? Really?" Without another word, he headed for a tree.

Curious, Nick watched as Shadow drew a sigil over the bark and spoke an incantation. The tree bark split apart and opened. Holding his breath, he waited to see these magical swords they were all so hot and bothered about.

But the moment it showed the inside of the trunk,

they realized Caleb was right. It was empty inside. There wasn't a single sword to be found.

Shadow and Caleb cursed in unison.

"Told you!"

Shadow shook his head in denial and cursed. "I don't believe this. You see where I kept them! No one else knew about this. No one else could get here to claim them, at all!"

Those words went through Nick as an awful bad feeling made his flesh crawl. "Here's a weird question." They turned to stare at him. "This would count as me learning their location, right? I mean, I don't really know, but I do. And if I've seen what I've seen and someone else saw what I just saw and then asked someone else who might know, then they could use my memory to find them, couldn't they?"

"What did he say?" Shadow scowled at him.

"Nick logic." Kody sighed before she explained it more clearly. "I think he's saying that Ambrose might have stolen them in the future."

"Close. I'm thinking Cyprian did." Nick gestured at the tree. "I just saw the location. Right? So

Ambrose would know the location as a memory. Which means Cyprian would have learned it when he got my memories after he killed me. He could have taken that to Grim or someone else and they might have figured it out if they mind-melded with him. At least that's a possibility. So in the future, he could steal the swords and then come back here with them and attack Caleb. Or come back in time and then steal them, then attack Caleb. Either way, he Bogarted the swords from my memories. Possible, right?"

Shadow cursed again—apparently he had trouble with that. "Well ... we just screwed up, didn't we? Why didn't someone tell me we had a time-traveling Malachai we had to guard against? That's new. What, boy? You get frisky in the future with a zeitjäger?"

"Uh, no. You seen what they look like? I don't ever want to get so drunk that I tap that. I would sooner die with my wizard powers intact, thank you very much. I will never touch a nip of alcohol or anything else. *Ever!*"

"Excuse me?" Nashira loudly cleared her throat. "They are quite nice, thank you very much! Much better looking than a Malachai!"

Caleb cleared his throat to keep them on topic. "And we still don't know for a fact that it was Cyprian who got his hands on the swords, folks," he reminded them. "Focus, escapees from ADD Academy."

Shadow jerked his chin at Nick. "His theory's the most sound. Bad as I hate to admit it. It explains how they could have found them."

"Which means those swords could now be in the hands of Noir and Azura. And if they are . . ."

Kody's words put a chill down the spine of them all. Noir and Azura were two of the gods of the original source of all evil. If those swords were in their hands . . .

It was a bad day for humanity. As the Source, they would have the ability to create new warriors for them. Warriors so powerful that no one could stand against them.

"We have to get those swords back."

Caleb laughed.

Until he realized she was serious. "Child, my entire army couldn't take down the Sephirii and believe me, we tried. All the Malachai together, couldn't defeat them. *They* tried. It was basically one bloody standoff every time we went to war against them. Which begs the question of who the hell was so stupid as to tell *you*, Shadow, to keep them?" He turned to glare at the man.

"And I repeat ... someone I trusted. Short list, that."

"You're an idiot."

"No arguments there. I used to hang out with you. Even worse, I followed you into battle, which says it all about my intellect and great mental abilities."

Nick stepped back out of Caleb's way. Given the expression on his face, he wasn't about to get between them in the event the demon started swinging. He knew that look and it never boded well for the person or demon receiving it.

"Before you two go World War III, can I ask something?" Now they were both giving *him* that glower. "What happened to the demons and swords that attacked you? Did you kill them all?"

"No. We barely beat them off. They were more intent on weakening us."

"Why?"

Caleb shrugged. "They're demons. They don't have to make sense."

Nick snorted at something he knew was bull. "Since when?"

"Since you never do."

He had a point. Still ... "Isn't this sending a flag up anyone's pole, other than mine?"

"He's right." Kody bit her lip. "They came at me and Nick, at the same time they attacked you. It was strategic. Why?"

"Divide and conquer." Caleb pulled the cloth away from his stomach to check his wound. "With those swords, they could have killed us. Yet they chose not to. You're right. There was some reason they pulled back."

A bad feeling went through Nick as he took Kody's hand. "What's your weakness?"

"You."

That single word made his stomach tighten and his heart light. But as sweet as it was, it wasn't what he needed right then. "Seriously, Kode. What are they trying to do with you?"

"While I'm technically dead, this body is living. It can be killed and I wouldn't be able to stay here. I'd have to leave you."

That thought tore him up inside. He couldn't imagine living without her. She was vital to him in a way he couldn't even begin to explain. Like breathing, only more important.

"What's the new Malachai's goal?" Nick whispered. Cyprian couldn't kill him without ending his own future. If Nick died now, he wouldn't be around to father him tomorrow. Kody was a different story. She technically didn't live in this time period, so she wasn't critical to Cyprian's future.

And while he'd seen Caleb in the future, it didn't mean his destiny couldn't be altered. His death wouldn't matter either.

Caleb sighed. "We know Sroasha wants you dead."

Nick nodded, well aware of that fact. "But what about Cyprian? What does he want here?"

"That is anyone's guess." Caleb passed another sullen glare at Shadow. "You should have destroyed every last one of those swords."

"Clearly I'm choking on regret."

"You're about to be choking on my fists."

"When did this escalate to violence?" Nick asked.

Caleb gestured at his stomach. "The moment I was stabbed. What part of me bleeding and my guts hanging out did you miss?"

Kody shook her head. "This bickering is pointless and Nick has something he should be doing."

"Yeah and I'm doing it. Protecting all of you."

She tsked at him. "You need to go and take care of the matter with Virgil. We've got this."

Nick didn't like the sound of that even a little bit. Nor did he trust in the universe enough that he believed for one yoctosecond it didn't plan to screw him over.

It always did.

"I don't like unsolvable puzzles."

Kody kissed his cheek. "We'll figure this out."

Growling low in his throat, Caleb took on his human appearance. "C'mon, Lord King Pain. Let's get this over with." He paused to glare at Shadow. "*You*, find out what happened. I'll be back to kick your butt later."

Shadow scoffed. "You better bring back up."

"Won't need it for your worthless hide."

He laughed. "I'll take that wager."

Without commenting, Caleb grabbed Nick and took him home.

Kody met Shadow's worried gaze the moment they were alone in his realm. "What are you hiding?"

"Certainly not the fact that I'm an idiot." He glanced over to Simi and then to Aeron. "'Course, *he* knows that."

Aeron laughed. "You haven't changed a bit."

"And you're hedging." She could feel it deep inside. He had an aura like Nick's. Both of them were handsome beyond belief, with a bashful confidence that said they'd been kicked enough to wear down their conceit. And both wore their cockiness as a mode of self-defense against a bitterly cruel world that ever sought to bring them to their knees. It made her protective of a man who was probably older than both her ancient parents.

"I'm just thinking that with those swords, in the right hands, they could breed new Sephirii."

"Would that be so bad?"

"Depends. Those swords were forged from the pit of the Source. The very essence of the universe is inside them. Their blades will cut through anything, and they will cut through anyone. With them, their wielders can kill gods."

"But the swords have to choose who wields them and they don't bond with just anyone, yes?"

"True, but the swords feed on blood. They thrive on it. In the hands of a Source god, such as Azura or Noir, or one who is familiar with them, such as Grim or Laguerre, they can be tricked to bond against their wills. Enslaved if you will."

"What happens then?"

Shadow's eyes turned sinister and his voice dropped a full octave. "You create a monster so vicious, it makes the Malachai look like a friendly puppy."

CHAPTER 5

N ick felt the jolt to his powers the moment he walked into the police station. It slapped him like Stone's stench after gym class. And left him just as feral and ready to fight.

Totally Pavlovian.

Primal. The Malachai blood inside him reacted to evil the way a hungry baby embraced candy. It salivated and drooled, wanting him to tear them apart and feast on it.

His breathing turned ragged.

Virgil, who stood almost eye level with him, paused. "You okay, buddy?"

Nick felt his lip involuntarily curl. It actually wanted him to go for Virgil's neck—which would be really stupid as Virgil wouldn't take that lying down. He'd fight and make it hurt.

Eyes widening ever so much, Virgil stepped back. "I'll take that as a no."

And just as Nick was about to go for his throat, he felt an unexpected peace rise up within him. One so sudden and overwhelming that it made him gasp and stopped him dead in his tracks.

Thinking it was Kody, he turned to find his mother rushing toward them. Before he could so much as blink, she latched on to him in a fierce bear hug that was so powerful, it felt like some gigantic beast had wrapped itself around him and not the tiny waif of a woman who barely reached the middle of his chest and weighed less than his right thigh.

A slight exaggeration on her weight. But really, his mom couldn't be more than a buck even after an all day bender at the Café Du Monde.

"My baby Boo! You okay?" The tears in her voice wrecked him.

"Fine, Ma." He squeezed her back gently so that he didn't hurt her.

She nodded. "Okay. I'm going to beat some sense into these *bracque crotte, mon petit garçon.* Anyone goes to jail for murder today, it'll be me and they'll have you over my dead body."

Now *his* eyes widened at her choice of words. While calling them a crazy turd wasn't technically profanity, it was so unusual for his mother to insult anyone that it shocked him.

Ruffling his hair, she kissed his cheek and turned toward Virgil. "Point me toward someone, anyone, so that I can kick their stupid butts and get my baby home. No one messes with my boy!"

Like him, Virgil towered over the much tinier Cherise Gautier. And even the vampire lawyer, Virgil Ward, stepped back in fear from her fury. "Yes, ma'am. Right this way."

As he led her away, Bubba stepped forward with a laughing grin. "That's right, fear the mighty

Chihuahua. Whoo, boy, your mama has been riled up since the moment they came by for you. And I am sure that officer is in therapy right now and will remain there for the rest of his life. I had no idea your mama knew that kind of language. Thank God, I'm not the one what ruffled her feathers. Remind me to *never* rattle her cage unless I make sure she's padlocked in it."

Nick snorted. "I'd be offended if it wasn't the truth. Love the woman, but her temper's like a head injury. It's hilarious only so long as it's happening to someone else."

"Yeah, that be about right." Bubba winked at him, then sobered. "How you holding up?"

"*Ça c'est bon, n'est pas?* Just a little baffled by this." Nick cringed as a cop came a little too close and eyed him like some Friday night hoodlum.

Bubba glanced around. "So where's the rest of your crew? Not like you to run solo."

"Caleb's on his way. Said he'd be here any minute. What about you? Who's babysitting Mark?"

Laughing again, Bubba scratched at his dark hair.

He was one of the few people Nick looked up to. Both figuratively and literally. But not by much. He probably had an inch on him in height. Muscle-wise, Bubba was a monster beast. As a former football player, he had the kind of body Nick would kill for. And unlike Acheron, Caleb and Kyrian, he wasn't lean. He was Terminator muscle. The kind that made even tough guys gulp and stand down.

Which was one of the reasons why Nick was agreeable for Bubba to date his mother. So long as the two of them were together, Nick knew no one would hurt his mom. Bubba was a fierce attack beast who'd tear them to shreds if they so much as grimaced in her general direction.

And Cherise Gautier had no fear of him whatsoever. Bubba was always respectful of her and was as easily cowed by the barking Chihuahua as Nick was.

He liked that quality in a man. It made him feel better about being scared of his mother.

"Mark's actually out on a date of his own."

Nick gaped at the last thing he expected to hear. Not that he should be surprised. Mark was a far cry from a mutant life form. It wasn't so much that Mark couldn't get a date as much as Mark disdained the hassle of dating. And his last relationship had ended so badly, the man had PTSD from it.

And burn scars.

"Really?"

Bubba held his hand up to swear by his statement. "Believe me, I'm as shocked as you are. I think he has a head injury from our last taping."

Nick burst out laughing at the reminder of their "survival tip" that had almost killed them both. While videoing an episode for their *Zombie Alert Network*, Mark had slipped and fallen from his chair, hit his head and knocked a rack of MRE's down on top of him. Somehow one of them had fallen in such a way that it'd set off a flare that then struck a display and almost set fire to Bubba's entire store.

"So who's he out with?"

"The nurse from the burn ward."

Snorting and shaking his head, Nick settled down into a nervous laugh. "He should probably marry this one. It'd save on the medical bills."

Bubba scoffed.

Suddenly, someone grabbed Nick from behind. Hissing in fury, he turned to punch them, only to find Caleb there. "Boy!" he snapped. "You're lucky I didn't take your manhood just then."

When Caleb didn't respond with something snotty, a bad feeling went through Nick. But this had to be Caleb. Otherwise it would trip his perspicacity and he'd see the truth of who and what this creature was.

Unless it's the other Malachai.

A smile twitched at the outer edges of "Caleb's" mouth—as if he were reading Nick's thoughts.

The Malachai took a step toward him at the same time Nick felt his mom at his back.

Unaware of the creature with them, she smiled at them both. "Hey Caleb, *mon beau-coeur.* I knew you couldn't be far behind my Boo." She stepped past Nick to hug him.

Nick started to protest until he saw the expression on "Caleb's" face. At first it was startled alarm that settled down to all-out shocked disbelief.

And then there was a longing, so profound that it choked him for the demon. It was obvious he'd never been hugged before and there was nothing quite like one of his mother's hugs. The closest thing Nick could compare it to was being wrapped in rose-scented sunshine. It warmed every part of the soul and could soothe any pain or ache in an instant.

No wonder my dad couldn't resist her. She never saw the bad in anyone. Not him. Not his father.

Not the creature whose eyes began to tear.

Right before they flashed red and his nostrils flared.

Clearing his throat, "Caleb" mumbled something, then ran for the door.

With a hurt look, his mother turned toward him. "Did I do something wrong? Is he okay?"

Leave it to his mother to quell the most horrific evil in all the known universes. Not with a fight or a shout.

With a simple hug.

"I think he had to whizz, Mom."

"Nicholas! I trained you better than that. I swear, boy! The things you do!"

He rubbed at his eyebrow. "What can I say, Ma? I'm not quite housebroken yet."

Bubba laughed. "You want me to beat him for you, Cher? Be glad to. Or worse, I can make him clean Mark's bathroom."

A smile broke across her face. "I'll just make him clean his. Trust me, there's no worse punishment. Have you seen the biohazard experiments he has growing on his sink?"

"Ah, gee! Now who's being mean?"

Virgil approached them with Kyrian and Acheron. All three of them had a satisfied gleam in their eyes. "Well that was so easy, I feel bad to bill you for it." He handed a piece of paper to Nick. "You're free to go. And I suggest you buy your mom dinner, kid. We should all have an advocate like her in our corners. Dang. I've never seen anyone set a judge back that fast, and so politely." He clapped Nick on the shoulder, then left them.

Even Kyrian was smiling enough that Nick caught

a flash of his fangs. "He's not joking. Your mom is quite the lady, kid. So glad I'm not the one who riled her."

Kyrian clapped him on the back. The moment he did, Nick was jerked out of his body. Time stood still.

No longer in the police station, he was far in the future. Back in what he'd prayed was once a nightmare.

He saw himself as the Malachai, leading his army of demons through a devastated New Orleans that was burning all around them. Explosions went off like a pyrotechnics show. The rumble of thunder mirrored their hunger and anger.

All that was left intact was St. Louis Cathedral.

Where the last of the humans in the city remained cowering.

No, not cowering. Preparing a last stand. Tabitha. Bethany. Amanda. Kyrian. Their daughter, Marissa. Their son who'd been named after Nick.

And Kody.

With their daughter.

Nick froze as he suddenly knew the faces he

hadn't known before. Even though he was outside the building, he could see them inside it. Feel their panic. And their bravery.

Kody's mother, Bethany—an Egyptian goddess— grabbed their daughter, Chastity, and placed her in Kody's arms. "We'll hold them back. Take her and run."

Kody hesitated. "That's not Nick! You know it's not."

"There's only one Malachai."

"And I know my husband. He would never attack us. It's not in him."

Tabitha sneered at her. "Then where is he? Huh? He was supposed to meet us here. Him *and* Caleb."

"Nick wouldn't do this."

"Ambrose would." Tabitha wiped the blood from her cheek. "We lost him to the beast."

Bethany cupped her daughter's cheek before she kissed her and then her grandbaby. "Stand strong. Be safe." She nudged her toward a tall, blond man who was the very image of Acheron. And by that, Nick knew he must be Kody's brother. "You two take care of each other. Protect each other's back and stay safe, whatever it takes. Love you!"

A tear slid down the man's face. "Love you, Mom. Dad would be proud, if he were here."

She choked on a sob as she gave her son and daughter a tumultuous smile. "Yes, he would. Now go! I'll hold a shield around you as long as I can."

Kyrian pulled his daughter away from the children she was trying to comfort and protect. "Marissa, go with them."

"No! I won't leave you to this!"

Kyrian's wife, Amanda, joined them so that she could force her daughter to obey. "Yes. No argument. I'm not about to watch you die!"

Marissa began to cry over her parents' orders before she nodded. She hugged Kyrian, then Amanda and Tabitha. Without a word, she followed Kody to the back door. She paused to look back at them and the longing ache in her eyes made Nick choke on his own sob.

And the moment she left the knave, the front door broke open, spilling demons into the church.

Nick saw himself leading the demons.

Until Caleb, in his own demon form, came flying in for the attack.

The moment Caleb was there, Ambrose caught him by the throat. And in that instant, Nick realized something. Something he'd missed in his previous nightmares and visions.

Caleb met his gaze and froze. "Who are you?"

In all the visions he'd had before, Nick had taken that to mean that his friend hadn't recognized the Malachai demon that had swallowed Nick whole. That he'd been baffled by Nick's actions that day.

This time ... *this* time, Nick saw it for what it really was.

Too late, Caleb realized that he wasn't Ambrose.

Like Kody, he saw the truth of the beast. That this Malacahi was an imposter, and that was what had caused the Malachai to kill him. Not for the fact that Caleb had failed to follow his orders, or kill Kyrian and the others.

Caleb had known the truth.

There was a second Malachai masquerading as Ambrose.

"Who are you?" he breathed, desperate to have an answer as to who the Cyprian Malachai really was. But at least he had the comfort of knowing that he, *Nick*, wasn't the beast who'd killed everyone he loved.

He was only the poor fool framed for it all.

"Nick?"

He heard Kyrian's voice off in the distance.

At first he thought it was the wind. Until he realized his boss was dragging him from his vision and back to where they'd been in the busy police station.

Blinking, Nick glanced around them. "Um, yeah, sorry. I just remembered an assignment I didn't finish. I'm going to be in all kinds of trouble at school tomorrow if I don't get it done."

With that, he bolted for the door, needing to find out more about what was going on.

Caleb was still MIA and that wasn't like his demon protector. He didn't even let Nick go to the bathroom alone. That meant, something bad was up for Caleb to be missing this long.

More fear went through him as he struggled to stay in the present. But his powers kept trying to drag him away to both the past and the future.

At the same time.

He felt like a boat that'd lost all moorings. All sense of time and place.

He couldn't even begin to ground himself.

I need Kody.

Just as he was sure he'd lost his mind completely, he heard something calling to him.

Not a person, though. He wasn't sure what it was.

This is so peculiar.

How could he stop it and ground himself so that he didn't keep floundering?

"I will always be here for you."

On the steps, outside the station, Nick froze at the voice. The spinning stopped so that he could see the street and the traffic. He was still in New Orleans. In his right time period. This was where he was supposed to be.

Cocking his head, he reached out with his powers.

His mom, Bubba, Acheron and Kyrian were still in the station. Talking about him, and how strange he'd been acting.

They weren't the ones who'd spoken, though. That wasn't what he'd heard. The voice had been familiar, yet not theirs.

He struggled to place it and couldn't.

"What is wrong with me?"

With no clue, he pulled his phone out and dialed Caleb.

He didn't answer.

Completely worried, he tried Kody.

Like Caleb, she ignored his call, too. He reached out with his powers.

They, too, failed him.

Yeah, this was all kinds of wrong. A chill went down his sprine.

Nick attempted to teleport and couldn't. His powers were weakened again. The other Malachai was draining him faster than he'd ever dreamed possible. No wonder his father had stayed in prison after his birth.

He totally understood Adarian's demented rea-
soning now. It was probably the only way his father
had been able to retain any power at all. In prison,
Adarian could suck the evil straight out of the other
inmates so that he'd be able to fight against the
never-ending stream of enemies out to end or enslave
him.

That was why he'd been so aggressive whenever
Nick's mother had brought him in to visit. Why he'd
wanted to see Cherise alone.

Why his father had gone insane the only time
they'd released him from jail during Nick's child-
hood. Unable to stay away from his mother, his
father had shown up at their door and attempted to
live with them.

That had been a giant disaster.

Even now, Nick was scarred by it. Adarian had
glared at him with so much hatred it'd left him forever suspicious of any stranger. The only people Nick
trusted innately were his mother and Menyara.

Everyone else had to prove themselves.

Repeatedly.

Heck, sometimes even they did.

A small part of him was still suspicious of Kody and Caleb. Even Kyrian. He couldn't help it. It was as innate as breathing.

And all from that one summer of his father stalking him like a spider in the dark. Of Nick waking up to find his father standing over him, Adarian's breathing ragged and his hands held out as if he were one step away from strangling him. Nick had told his mother then that he'd seen his father's eyes glowing red.

"Nicky! Boo! You're imagining things. It's all them games you play with your friends and the movies you watch. What have I told you about that? Stop sneaking up to see them! You're too bright to believe in such nonsense."

It wasn't that. More, it came from the fact that his father whispered, "I hate you," under his breath anytime Nick ventured too close. That his father had hated him for making him weak and for draining his powers.

Then the insanity had come. His father had gone

on a killing spree, claiming there were demons after him.

Saddest part?

Adarian wasn't lying or delusional. Those were real demons who'd been after his father, trying to end him. But normal humans didn't believe in such things.

And the nondelusional part had been proven when a psychologist had deemed him sane enough to stand trial and be sentenced for consecutive life sentences for those murders. Because while humans refused to believe in the kinds of demons Nick fought, they did believe in the kind of demon they assumed his father had been for slaughtering "humans".

Yeah, it was a messed up world.

Even then, Nick's mom had shown compassion for the monster who'd been unleashed on an unsuspecting world, and hadn't hated him over it. But, that was her nature. She was born from the truest light. A creature of such innocence that she couldn't see the uglier side of humanity, no matter what was shown or unleashed on her.

Or apparently demons of any kind. Not even when they were right in front of her, and after she birthed one.

It was as impossible for her as for Nick to believe that Stone at school had a heart, or any semblance of decency. Instead, Nick always saw the evil in everyone around him. No matter how hard they tried to hide it. That was his "gift."

"Are you afraid yet?"

Nick went ramrod still at the disembodied voice. "I fear nothing." He never had.

"Good. That makes it more fun."

Suddenly, he was grabbed from behind and yanked into darkness.

CHAPTER 6

"Rubati?"

At the sound of Monakribos's voice, the warrior demon set aside the sword she was sharpening and stood to greet him. The fire was almost out now. Strange, but she'd lost all track of time while she'd been working on preparing her weapons for the upcoming inspection. Because Kree had put his reputation on the line to get her into the guard, the last thing she'd wanted was to embarrass him. So she'd been even more careful and studious about tending her weaponry and making sure to do nothing to cause him to regret his decision to back her.

She thought too much of him for that.

"In here, my lord." She quickly smoothed her hair and straightened her burgundy leather uniform at the sound of his approaching footsteps on the black marble floor.

Ru was just reaching for the door latch when he pushed it open, almost striking her with the ornate iron. Nervously, she stepped back with a gasp.

He drew up short. "Sorry. I didn't realize you'd be right on the other side."

Any thought of a response died on her tongue as she caught sight of his handsome Malachai form. Incredibly sexy and muscular, he towered over her and made her feel tiny and petite. Something hard for the majority of males to do as she was taller than most, and rather muscular.

He flashed an adorable smile at her. One that was framed by an unbelievable set of deep dimples. "Charonte got your tongue?"

She felt the heat creep over her face at his teasing question. He was ever unexpected and flippant. And something about him always left her breathless and hot. "Did you need something?"

The humor in his eyes died instantly. "Aye. There's a rumor that we're about to go to war."

"War?" Her blood rushed through her veins in eager excitement. It was, after all, what their kind lived for. What they'd been bred to do. She would welcome such a task with both arms.

He nodded. "My mother and her siblings are at each other's throats."

"There's nothing new about that."

"This is different. I hear it in her voice when she speaks. They've had enough of Verlyn, Rezar and Cam, and their dictates. And Lilith is making it worse. Pitting them against each other. Soon, they'll declare it and this world will burn down around all sentient beings. I fear what will be left when they're done with it."

"I will be ready."

Heat flared in his eyes. "I don't want you ready,

Ru. I want you safe." He took her hand into his and led it to his heart. "And before you say anything, I know you're capable of protecting yourself and reigning down entrails of any who dare attack you. It's not an indictment against your skills. This is a matter of my fear and feelings. I couldn't live if something happened to you because of my mother and her warring nature."

"I don't understand."

A slow smile spread over his face. "I love you, Rubati. I don't think I knew how to breathe until the day you stumbled into my worthless life. Please come and fight only by my side so that I can make sure you stay strong and allied throughout all battles . . . "

Those words echoed around Nick's head as Nick slammed into a dark, mossy wall. That memory of his ancestor felt like someone had ripped it from his mind to make it real. It was crystal clear as if it were his own meeting with her he witnessed. As if it'd happened to him this very morning.

He *felt* it.

More than that, Monakribos appeared suddenly in front of him. Larger than life and in full armored Malachai form. A living, breathing monster.

He was even larger than he'd appeared in the vision. More clear and terrifying with the same swirling black and red skin that Nick had in his Malachai form.

Nick felt his jaw go slack at the ferocity of the beast. Since he'd never seen himself in his demonic form, he'd had no idea just how massive they really were. How much evil they exuded.

No wonder other creatures were so skittish.

And since they inherited the powers, knowledge and strength of all their predecessors, his Ambrose form would be even more intimidating and fierce than this one.

Dang!

There was no other reaction to have.

Duly quelled, he swallowed hard as he tilted his head up to stare into the flaming red eyes that seared him. For the first time ever, he was grateful to have been spared seeing his dad like this. No doubt that would have given him nightmares for all eternity. "Are you real?"

Monakribos snorted. "I would have thought we'd have gained more intelligence over time." He shook his head in disappointment. "Pity, we got dumber."

"Hey now! I'm not the one who got us into this mess. So don't be pulling that attitude on me, boy. If there's an idiot between us, you're the one hogging it."

"At least you're not a coward." He lifted one clawed hand to wipe at his mottled red and black chin before he narrowed those menacing eyes at Nick. A tic started in his jaw. "So why have you summoned me?"

"Didn't know I had." Nick scowled as he considered that possibility. "Didn't know I could."

"Only in a time of crisis."

Well that explained it, then. This was definitely that. And it made him wonder when he'd picked up that new skill. 'Cause he'd never had it before. "In that case . . . yeah, I could definitely use some help."

Monakribos reached into the brown leather pouch at his side that was attached to his sword belt, and pulled out a small silver flask. He held it out toward Nick. "Drink this and I'll be able to answer any question you have."

Without thinking, Nick reached for it. Yet the moment his hand brushed the metal, a bad feeling went through him. *What are you doing?*

You don't trust anyone.

He never had. And for good reason.

Don't take candy from a stranger. And for the love of the gods, never, ever accept a treat from a Malachai!

Yeah, that had to be written in the great, grand hall of special stupidity. What kind of friggin' moron would take anything from a demon and ingest it? For all he knew, it could be anything. Drano. Snot.

Or something a lot worse. After all, drinking blood from a cup was what had gotten Acheron made into a Dark-Hunter and tied to Artemis . . .

Yeah. Beware the cup.

Holding his hands up, Nick stepped back. "Um, yeah. I don't think so."

Monakribos gaped in disbelief, "Pardon?"

"You can pardon all you want to, buddy. Do-si-do,

too. Even dance a little Cajun fais do-do and play some zydeco. Changes nothing. There some things Nick Gautier don't do. Lie to Big Bubba Burdette. Disrespect my mama. Miss any Holy Day of Obligation. Stand behind Acheron's back at any given time, and enter Kyrian's bedroom without knocking until he yells at me. And never, *ever*, will I fight Simi for food or cheat on my girl. Or be one minute late for a date."

He jerked his chin toward the flask. "And the devil will be eating on some icicles before I take a swig of something a stranger hands to me, especially one of your ilk and out of a magic flask. 'Cause I know what happened to Alice and I don't mean Cooper. For all I know, you're gonna roofie me and I'll wake up naked some place weird, without my clothes, and with some awkward photos posted online that I'll have to try and explain to my girl and my mama. No thank you, very much. I have little enough dignity as it is. Don't need any less."

The demon scowled even more. "Did you suffer a head injury?"

"Probably. Stone's been known to slam me into a number of lockers at inconvenient times. Wouldn't be surprised if he knocked out all my brains at some point."

Monakribos tried to push the flask into his hand. "There's nothing wrong with the water."

"Then you drink it, Mister Mad Hatter Rabbit. If you don't shrink or 'shroom from it, I'll believe you."

"What is wrong with you?"

Nick snorted. "Oh, that's an extremely long, *long* list. At least according to my guidance counselor. I start naming everything off and we'll be here all day."

The Malachai rolled his eyes. "Do you want answers or not?"

"I do."

"Then drink it."

Yeah, right ... Nick had missed his stupid pills that morning.

All of them.

There was no way he was about to cooperate on this. "Nah, that's all right. I'd really rather put my head in a blender and turn it on liquify." And his dander was seriously kicking up, along with his Cajun obstinance and even more suspicion. "You an all-powerful beastie. Why do I have to drink that for you to answer a simple question? Seriously, bruh. That don't even make sense in my mind."

In fact, it only made him angrier. The color on his own skin darkened as his eyes began to glow. He could actually feel his eyes radiating. No doubt they now matched Monakribos's.

Nick was so distracted by his fury that he failed to notice that the Malachai had summoned a few "friends" to join their party.

Friends who'd surrounded him and were now taking up positions that were less than nice. In fact, they grabbed him and pulled him toward the ground.

Growling, he fought against them as hard as he could.

"Hold him! We need to get the water down his throat!"

Nick's eyes flared even more at those words. *I knew it!* He didn't know what water was in that flask or why it was important, but . . .

If they wanted it in him, then he wasn't about to oblige them. So he clamped his lips and eyes shut tight with every bit of his natural-born stubbornness that had caused every teacher he'd ever had to curse and question his parentage.

His heart pounded against his breastbone like a sledgehammer. They slammed him against the ground and held him there while he fought and twisted, trying his best to throw them off. Yeah, no toddler had anything on him! He'd give two-year-olds everywhere a lesson in tantrums.

One of them clamped a hand over his mouth and nose, trying to pry his lips apart.

Nick choked. Even so, he managed to keep his lips shut, but it was almost impossible.

Growling and kicking, he fought even harder.

With every power he'd been taught, he lashed out and still they rode him like a mechanical bull. Determined and painful.

Caleb! Simi! Xev! He screamed out with his telepathy. His muscles burned. His soul wanted vengeance. Every molecule of his being was in utter agony.

And still no one answered.

Never had he felt so alone. But that didn't stop him from fighting. There were times in life when you had no choice. You had to fight alone. No help came. No matter had much you needed it. How desperately you wanted it.

You were bitterly alone. Nick knew that better than anyone.

Which made fighting for yourself all the harder.

And all the more necessary.

Because while it was easier to fight for others, the hardest fight would always be for yourself and for your own personal matters. To fight for what was right. To fight for what *you* needed. Your principles. *Your* causes. And what you knew to be the truth.

To stand alone in the maelstrom.

Those were the times that mattered most. The times when there was no one around to see your private battles. When it was just you and your integrity. Your dignity. When you knew you had to stand your ground or be trampled over.

Let no one take you down.

You stand and you fight until the end! Not for fanfare, or for applause or laurels, but because you know what's right and what's wrong. Never fight because you have an audience or to gain esteem or notoriety. You fight for what matters—for the right things in life. Truth. Honesty. Dignity. Let no one steal, lie or cheat. You keep what you earn and never allow anyone to run over you because of the lies they tell others. And the lies others are so willing to believe about you.

That was what his mother had taught him. What she'd shown him all the times she'd held her head high, in spite of all the people who'd sneered at her for the choices she'd made where he was concerned.

Right was right. You soldiered on through the pain of life, others be damned. All lies be damned. Past the betrayal and the deceit. The hopelessness. No matter how dark it might seem. No matter how defeated you might feel at the moment.

Where there was breath, let there be fight.

And there was a lot of fight in him.

Forever.

Rise through the pain, Nicky-Boo. No matter how

dark the night. Or how bitter the storm, light always finds a way through the densest clouds to shine again. Remember that, and hold it tight to your chest, whenever you feel defeated. Whenever you want to give up. Lift one fist and one finger to the sky, and defy them all to the bitter end!

That was the lesson he'd learned from Menyara and Acheron. *Let no one steal your light with their lies or their cruelty. Shine on, through it all. Shine in spite of their hatred. In spite of the hurt they give. Let them all choke on your light until it blinds them and washes away whatever meanness they're intent to spew.*

Tomorrow, no one will remember what cruel thing they said, but they will remember how you held your head high during the storms. They will remember the brightness of your smile and the way you laughed while they tried to bring you down. Let your laughter be the beacon that warms the world.

And with that thought, his powers surged. Like a tidal swell, rising up through a storm. It toppled over and lifted Nick until he was ripped away from the demons.

One minute, they had him and the next, he was free of their claws and lying crumpled on the floor of his bedroom.

Safe from their stinging attacks.

Dazed, and completely disoriented, Nick lay on the ground, trying to get his bearings. He wasn't even sure what time it was. Not even the day of the week.

Or the month.

It was the strangest disoriented feeling.

Had he broken some time-travel law? He had no idea at this point—just about anything seemed possible. This had been the oddest day of his life. And given the weirdness he'd been coping with, that said a lot.

"You okay?"

Blinking, he turned his head to find Xev in the corner of his room, staring at him. Dressed all in black, he was holding a small pad and appeared to be drawing—Xev's newest hobby he'd developed lately to pass a good time and stay sane.

"Um ... not sure." Nick felt at his face and hair,

which were dry and seemed to be normal. "I was under attack."

Xev arched a brow. "By?"

"Demons. The other Malachai. At least I think that's what happened, but anymore ... who the heck knows. Just once I'd like for it to be a super-model out to find some teen for an experiment, you know?"

Xev set his pad aside and scooted closer. "Where's Caleb?"

"Don't know. He abandoned me." Nick grimaced. "*You* abandoned me."

"You didn't call."

"Yeah, I did. No one answered."

Xev drew his brows together into a stern frown. "I would never have ignored you. You know that."

He was right. Even more overprotective than his mom, Xev would never ignore a cry of help. If Nick so much as burped, Xev tried to perform the Heimlich on him.

Still confused and disoriented, Nick sat down on his bed and tried to get a handle on everything.

"This day . . . it's been one of the more peculiar ones. That I definitely gotta say. Everyone's been under attack."

"How so?"

Another bad feeling went through Nick at the way Xev said that. He wasn't acting like his hypersensitive great-granddad. While this dude might have Xev's black hair and hazel brown and green eyes, this wasn't right. He was a little too chill for how the ancient being normally took such news.

"You look a little glum. Been missing Inari?"

Xev nodded.

Nick shot off the bed and bolted for the door as he realized this wasn't Xev, but rather the other Malachai—or some other imposter. Inari was the demon who'd suckled Xev—the stepmother demon he hated.

Myone had been his wife he pined for. And while Cyprian might have known their names, he wouldn't have known the difference between them unless he spent time around Xevikan.

Then no one would mistake the two women and

what they meant to the surly god who was devoted to one, and disgusted by the other.

A light flashed in Cyprian's eyes as he realized his mistake. "You're a quick one."

"That I am. And you are not." Nick struggled against the door that wouldn't open and his powers that refused to let him teleport out of here. "Why are you doing this?"

"Because I need you to forget!"

"Why?"

"You're screwing up everything!"

"Me? You're the one killing innocent people!"

"I'm cleaning up *your* mess!"

"I'm not the one who started this!" Nick attacked him. The two of them went at it with everything they had. Never had Nick wanted to kill anyone so badly. He was sick of it all. Sick of Cyprian copying all of his friends, and pretending to be them at every turn.

This was crap and they both knew it.

"Get your own friends and life!" Nick growled at him. "What is wrong with you!"

"It's not fair for you to have what I want! For you to be so loved and cherished when I'm not!"

"Dude! Then learn to be lovable and not a psychopath! Practice being a decent human being and stop stealing everything I have. You don't get stuff just because you want it and you demand it like some two-year-old. It's about finding your own way, not taking someone else's life. Be yourself. Not a bad copy of what you stole. Step out of the shadows where you hide from everyone in fear, and into the light. Have the courage to stand by your own convictions, and walk your own path. Do your own thing! You can never build yourself up while you're tearing everyone else down and trying to catch up to them."

"Then give me what I want!"

Nick shook his head. "You have to earn your own way, dude. This is *my* life. This is *my* world and *my* family. For that, I will fight you until Lucifer is working in an ice plant."

"And I'm your son!"

"I didn't create you. You were ripped from me

and made, without my knowledge or consent. That's entirely different!"

Cyprian kicked him back. "I hate you!"

"Why? Dude, I never did anything to you. Seriously. If you want to hate, at least give me a chance to screw you over first."

Shrieking, he ran for him.

Nick caught him and held him against his chest. His Malachai powers were draining out more and more. There was nothing he could do. If he didn't get away from Cyprian, he'd be as helpless as a kitten soon.

And still Cyprian pounded against him with so much anger that Nick couldn't fathom it. What could he have done to cause this much animosity in someone he didn't know? All he'd ever done was live his life on his own terms. Be himself.

It wasn't his fault Cyprian's mom had created him against Nick's wishes and without his knowledge.

His ears began to buzz as the last of his powers surged and he saw himself in the past. Saw the night that he'd first met Kyrian.

Life had seemed so easy then. Stay clean. Stay off drugs. Keep his grades up. Don't miss work.

The only people out to kill him had been his mom whenever he left the toilet seat up.

Madaug whenever he forgot to complete a homework assignment they'd been given as a joint project, and Brynna for not realizing she had a crush on him.

When had life gotten so complicated?

Then he saw the future—not for long, just the tiniest flash of clairvoyance. And he understood the truth of the violent act that had created Cyprian.

Not one Nick had done against Cyprian's mother.

An act they had committed against Nick . . .

For all Malachai were created in violence to do violence.

Holy crap!

That was one nightmare he hadn't seen coming. Them attacking him. *This is what they're trying to protect.* Why they wanted him to forget his powers and forget everything.

His vision dimmed. *You can't die. You have to remember this!*

But then, that wasn't the end game.

I won't be manipulated!

With a feral growl, Nick dug deep and used the last of his powers to teleport into darkness.

CHAPTER 7

His mind reeling from the newfound knowledge, Nick tumbled through the darkness. The rustling sound was deafening. Like birds flapping through the night. He felt the wind against his skin as he sought once more to get his bearings.

Until he struck solid ground.

Out of the darkness came a lilting voice.

"Do you know me?"

Nick froze at someone who seemed familiar and at

the same time foreign. He glanced around the dense forest he didn't recognize. "Where are you?"

His breath caught as the shimmering Sephiroth woman stepped out of the shadows to his right. Dressed in gilded armor and with black braided hair, she was remarkably beautiful with gold, gossamer wings. Even in height to him, he knew her from the sketches Xev had drawn in his bedroom.

Myone. The mother of Jared—Nick's archnemesis and grandfather. The one warrior who'd betrayed his entire army to the side of evil in an effort to save what he'd believed was his father's life. However, Jaden wasn't Jared's father. Jaden was Xevikan's father— Jared's grandfather.

A lie told to keep Jared and Xev alive and safe from those who would have killed Myone had they learned that she, the pinnacle of all good and the beloved leader of the Kalosum army, had been seduced by the son of ultimate evil—Xev. It wouldn't have mattered that Xev had married her first. Or how much they loved each other. Or that they were completely devoted to one another—indeed, that devotion would have made it all the worse for them, because no one would have ever trusted Myone again as she would have been seen as totally corrupt. For they would have only believed that Xev brought her down to his level. Not that she raised him up to hers.

Which was the truth. While she was beyond corruption, for her alone, Xev would do anything. She had given him his soul and she was the one and only thing in the universe he would never betray or cause harm to.

But instead of believing that Xev could be saved, all that would have mattered to the others was that neither she nor her child could ever be trusted, because Xev's blood was demonic. In their minds, that bit of evil would override any amount of good.

Always.

Nick knew better. He understood exactly how much sway such kindness had. How much pull his mother and Kody had over him. It wasn't something that could be explained.

Only experienced.

How sad an indictment against so many that they

couldn't have faith in others to know just how solid such honesty was. That their hearts were so corrupt that they refused to believe creatures like Xev and him were above their pettiness. Yet they were.

And so they were forced into hiding. Forced into lies they didn't want to live or tell.

Not because they were wrong or *they* couldn't be trusted. Because others refused to see the good inside them. Because others refused to *believe* the goodness inside them.

Since they lacked it themselves, they refused to see it in anyone else. But denying it didn't kill it. It just made it all the more special and rare.

And for that reason, Jared had made a deal with the Source of all evil to spare his grandfather's life. And Jaden had enslaved himself in an effort to save Jared so that he wouldn't be killed, along with his army.

Both betrayed by the gods they'd trusted to deal fairly with them.

And Myone had paid dearest of all. She'd lost everything in the end. Her son, her husband and her life.

For that, Nick could weep for them all.

Now, the Sephiroth warrior stood before him, her scarlet cape draped around a lithe, armored body. It was held back in places from her shoulders by a quiver of arrows and a gilded sword belt.

"I know you," Nick breathed.

Indeed, she was a hard one to miss with her gold-kissed skin and shining gold wings. Her braided black hair reflected blue in the dim light. Every exquisite feature was perfection. No wonder Xev had been willing to die for her. That he'd suffered a fate worse than death to protect her and their son, when he'd stepped aside and allowed her to marry his father and pretend that his child belonged to his father so that no one would ever suspect the truth.

That was the purest form of altruism and love.

Not once had Xev ever breathed a word of it for fear of causing either his ex-wife or child harm. Nick couldn't imagine the pain and agony Xev had known every day of his life, and he was grateful for that.

Without a word, Myone watched him curiously.

Her shining gold vambraces held an ornate design that designated her as the leader of her Sepherii brethren—their kyra. As did the epaulettes of her uniform. She carried herself like a fierce warrior, even though she was all feminine grace.

The only piece of jewelry on her body was an out-of-place masculine necklace. One Nick knew belonged to Xev. And only because it was a match for the one Xev wore that symbolized her dainty feathered Sephiroth wing, unlike her roughened bat-shaped demon piece. How odd that no one had ever realized what those two necklaces meant and why the two of them wore them.

Her lips trembled as she approached Nick. "You are the only one who has been kind to my Dary. For that I can't thank you enough."

It took him a second to remember that Xev's real name was Daraxerxes, especially since Xev never used it. "Um, yeah, I guess."

A tear fell down her cheek. "You are not as the others of your kind."

"That's what they tell me."

She smiled sadly. "And they would be right. Do you know where we are?"

"Not a friggin' clue."

She laughed. "It is a place that never was. A land of where there can never be. Neither here nor there. It's where we're sent to bleed."

Dang, she was starting to sound like Nashira now. Made him almost want to reach for his grimiore to see if he'd left it at home. "That makes no sense whatsoever."

"You're the Malachai, Nick. You know all things. Just look inside and trust in yourself. The answers you seek are already there. You know them. You just don't want to face them. It doesn't matter how many polls you take, or friends you ask. The answers never change. They're already in your heart. You just need to believe in the truth. Believe in yourself. Have confidence."

That was easier said than done. He was too used to being told he didn't have enough experience. Enough sense. That he was too young to have a clue about anything.

Now she was telling him to trust an instinct he doubted.

It was as confusing as his mother teaching him to walk and talk and then the moment he started asking questions about things she didn't want to answer, telling him to sit down and shut up.

Life. It really needed to come with some kind of instruction booklet. Or at least a help manual. 'Cause most days, it just baffled the crap out of him.

And before he could get a handle on it, a zeitjäger appeared to his left.

Nick's eyes widened at the creepy plague doctor whose bandages were covered in blood.

He held his hands up at the creature as it eyed him suspiciously. "Hey, bruh, not the one who broke your time sequence. You're sniffing up the wrong Malachai here." He gestured off to the side. "Head that way. Over there. Off with you. Go on . . . Find the other dude."

Instead, it approached him slowly.

Fantastic. Just what he wanted for Christmas. Along with a head injury and thorough degutting.

Nick didn't move, but he did eye the grisly adamantine sickle the beast carried—'cause that was just gooey and gross. He could have done without the bloody stage theatrics. "You know, I heard Ozzy was in town, looking for some new backup singers. You might want to try out . . . " Nick's voice trailed off as the creature gave him a menacing glare that said he wasn't amused. "Never mind."

Cocking its head, it studied Nick even more intently.

Nick studied him back with the same level of intensity. But this time, he wasn't afraid of the creature. He was beginning to understand it.

They weren't enemies.

Nor were they allies.

He wasn't really sure what they were. At least not until the thing finally spoke in a chilling, broken voice.

"Cyprian is after you." The zeitjäger's voice was brittle and harsh—like an old man who'd smoked too many packs of cigarettes.

"Pardon?"

"He has fractured this time and will destroy it all. You have to reset it."

"How?"

The zeitjäger opened his hand and manifested a glowing skull in his palm. It wasn't quite human, but rather demonic in nature, with tusks that protruded over the jaw, toward the eye sockets. Nick knew instinctively that it belonged to Monakribos. Though how the zeitjäger had come into possession of it, he wasn't really sure he wanted to know.

"You will know what to do, when the time comes."

"Y'all all keep saying things like that. But really . . . I'm about as useful as the G in lasagna."

It made a peculiar noise that some might consider a laugh. Nick wasn't sure.

"Reset the sequence and reclaim your fate. *You* are the Malachai."

Nick wasn't so sure about that. "And if my fate is to destroy the world?"

"Have you so little faith in yourself?"

He had a point.

Nick took the skull. It had an odd warmth to it. One that didn't make a lot of sense. "Does Cyprian have to be born?" If he could stop that, it seemed like the easiest fix.

The zeitjäger hedged a bit. "Perhaps. But the real question is, does he have to hate you when he's born?"

Nick hesitated as that opened up a whole realm he hadn't even considered. His mind whirled with entirely new prospects. "You're saying that I can save him?"

But that didn't make sense. There could only be one Malachai.

Right?

"The future is never set, Ambrose. It changes with every decision we make. Until the day you die, it is ever in flux. Pith point, or not."

And with that, he vanished.

Stunned, Nick turned to stare at Myone. His breath caught as two images went through his head simultaneously. One was of Xev with Myone. It was a tender embrace with him standing behind her, holding her close in the shadows of her ancient balcony. Both dressed in their battle armor. It was a stolen moment, and the expression on their faces seared him with the depth of how much they loved each other. With the fact that they both knew what they had couldn't last and that if anyone found out, it would end them both.

Even so, they had forged a love that still haunted them. One that continued to burn inside Xev. Against all odds and all enemies.

Against all punishments.

Society be danged.

The second image was of the two of them on a battlefield, riddled with arrows and wounds. Both of them dying. Weeping, Myone had held Xev against her while he, weakened by blood loss, had tried to wipe the blood from her face.

Rather than allowing him to die at peace with his love, his enemies had seized him from her arms and dragged him away, even as the life had faded from her eyes. She'd been left to die alone on the battlefield.

Xev's fate had been far crueler. They'd denied him the release of death, and enslaved and tortured him for all eternity.

Because he'd dared to fall in love.

Forced to live without her, and to serve the ones who'd caused her death. No chance to reunite in spirit with his love. No chance to help his son or to spare either of them from their own damnation.

Xev had been sold by his own father into an eternity of torture. A blood slave to the Malachai and to whatever demons the Malachai chose to feed him to.

In that moment, Nick felt even more horrible for the two of them. "I'm sorry, Myone."

"For what?"

"For what was done to you and to Xev. And Jared."

A sad smile curved her lips before she walked toward Nick. "It's all right, Nicholas. We couldn't have asked for a more beautiful great-grandson. I'm glad I got to meet you." And with that, she kissed his cheek and vanished.

Nick couldn't breathe as his own tears choked him. He'd never met his grandparents before. Never mind his great-grandparents. Therefore, he'd never dreamed of what his great-grandparents would be like.

To have finally met her . . .

His Malachai wings shot out of his back against his will. But instead of being their usual black color, they were as gold as Myone's had been.

Confused, he stared at them, wishing someone was here to explain that to him.

What's happening to me?

Why was he having these visions? Were they real?

Had he fallen down a real rabbit hole? Or worse, had he drank some of that water? It was possible some had gone into his mouth. He still didn't know what had been in that bottle.

What the heck is going on?

Worse, the peculiar rustling began again. Only this time, he had a weird inkling about what was causing it.

No ...

It couldn't be.

Titling his head back, he glanced up at the oddly colored sky, and listened closely. The off-landscape tilted again and the whispering voices echoed.

You're losing your mind.

Was he? 'Cause what he was beginning to suspect would make an awful lot of sense.

And yet ...

Nick held his hand up and poked at the air. It sizzled.

Oh yeah, that wasn't normal. Even in his screwed up existence. Swallowing hard, he reached into his pocket and pulled out his hematite pendulum. *Please let me be wrong.*

Yet knowing he wasn't, he pricked his finger and drew a bead of blood. He held his breath and then drew with it.

Instead of falling on the ground as it should have, the air absorbed it and it glowed as bright as the lights on Takeshi's grid.

More than anything, that confirmed Nick's suspicions.

He *was* right.

Some how, some way, he'd been sucked into his own grimoire.

CHAPTER 8

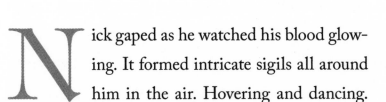

N ick gaped as he watched his blood glowing. It formed intricate sigils all around
him in the air. Hovering and dancing.
Reforming into intricate designs ...

And to think, his mom had once blistered his butt
for painting on the walls at home. She'd have a fit if
she ever saw this.

"Well ain't this the thing ... "

Now the question was how had he gotten here?

More importantly, how did he go about getting

out? Last thing he wanted was to be stuck in this book forever, like someone else he knew.

His stomach drew up tight at the thought. Yeah, that really was the last thing he needed. To be stuck in here a few thousand centuries like her.

"Nashira!"

She didn't answer. Not that he really expected it. Even when she'd been trapped in the book like this, she'd been less than forthcoming with information. And not always swift to answer his summons.

But at least he knew his blood was still relatively powerful here and that it could continue to perform spells and sigils. That at least explained why he was able to channel the things he'd been channeling, and have some of these less than fun delusions. The book allowed him to see his past and a part of the future. It was a guidebook of sorts. So this was all beginning to make a little bit of sense to him now.

Yeah, it was a guidebook that had been passed down through generations. From one Malachai to another . . .

"Dad," that one word left his lips before he could stop it.

What are you doing, Nick! Your father hated you. Have you lost your mind?

Maybe, but his dad had also given his life for them. So maybe, just maybe, he wasn't a total lunatic for thinking his dad might help him now.

Maybe . . .

After all, his dad had loved his mother. Maybe that love would overcome Adarian's innate hatred of him. Miracles were possible.

Nick stood in indecision for several minutes before he decided to take a chance he prayed didn't come back and bite him on the butt. Like they normally did.

'Cause out of all the idiotic ideas he'd had over the years, this was the granddaddy boss leader.

Power up, bruh.

Closing his eyes, he summoned what little was left of his strength.

"What have you done now?"

Yeah, he'd know that deep, guttural hate-filled tone anywhere.

"Good to see you, too, Dad."

Adarian materialized so that he could stand there with malevolent red eyes that seared him to the core of his rotten soul. "Didn't I tell you to watch your mother?"

"You did, and I'm trying."

"Then why are you trapped here where you can't help her, huh?"

"I wish I knew."

Hissing, Adarian took a step forward, then froze. He cocked his head as if he heard something strange. "You have no idea what you're doing, do you?"

That was one massive understatement of fact. Of course he didn't. Never had. And at this point, he'd wager that he never would. Least the odds were looking that way.

"Was hoping you'd have some idea on that. I'm thinking we're in the Malachai's grimoire. Am I right?"

With a dark scowl, Adarian held his hand up to glare at it as if it were some foreign object. "How is this even possible?"

"Again, clueless. Was hoping you could enlighten me as to what would suck me in here."

Adarian grabbed him by his arm and yanked him up against his chest. Then flew with him up toward the dark sky.

Nick started to protest, but he was too weak to break his father's hold. Something that really concerned him. "Hey!"

"Stop struggling!"

Normally, he'd never obey anyone who held him like this, yet there was a note in his father's voice that said he needed to listen. And when they reached the outer edge of the paper, Nick saw why.

There was a thin membrane that allowed him to see through the worlds in a way he'd have never thought possible.

Similar to Takeshi's map, this was like a starchart to the multiverse.

Nick gaped as he tried to make sense of it all. "What is this?"

"Everything." His father's wings flapped loudly in his ears, rushing a cold wind around them.

"I don't understand."

"The grimoire is the lifeblood of our species, boy. It's all and nothing. What is and was and could be. The darkest of magick, it was forged from the living skin cells of Cam by Lilith during the Primus Bellum and given to Monakribos so that he could defeat the Kalosum."

Nick groaned in frustration as he tried to follow that. But it still didn't make sense. "You've still lost me on this one, old man."

Hissing, he spoke to Nick through gritted fangs. "The grimoire is a living book, you imbecile. Made from the flesh of Lilith's sister. She hated her siblings for what they'd done to her and her children. For the curse they placed on her that turned her children in to monsters, so our book was her revenge on them. Since her children couldn't attack the Source and lacked the ability to kill them, she was hoping the first Malachai would use her knowledge and its powers against her siblings to destroy them for her."

"Why didn't he?"

"He never had the chance." Adarian pulled Nick

188

to a page where a pair of lips were imprinted on the ancient vellum. "Before Monakribos could use it against them, Cam had Rubati place a note to her husband in the book and seal her letter with a bit of her blood that binds her to it. It's part of her, too. After that, he couldn't bring himself to destroy this bit of her being. Like you, it now contains a balance between them and so it has become our guide. A conscience of sorts for our species that confuses more than it helps. It's Rubati's pure soul that keeps us from using the book's knowledge to destroy the world. It's also why we have to keep it near us. Why we can't be without the cursed thing."

"Is that why you put Nashira in it?"

He nodded. "I was hoping her hatred of me would override Rubati's spell and allow me to either destroy the book or use it as it was intended. Instead, she only vexed me more." He shoved at Nick. "Like *you*!" Adarian sneered the word, yet this time Nick felt the love that undercut his father's derision.

"So how do I save Mom? Please, you have to help me figure out a way to do it."

Sadness darkened Adarian's eyes, turning them orange. "Have you seen that night?"

Nick shook his head. "I can't."

"It's not what you think. And it's not what you know."

He scowled at his father's cryptic words. "For the love of God, can you not tell me a straight answer? What is that supposed to mean?"

Adarian roared in anger. His breathing labored, he grabbed Nick's shoulders and forced him to meet his gaze. "If you want to fix this, forget what you think you know about your life and the future, moron. Find Cyprian before he finds you, and stop him. It's that simple!"

"How?"

"The same way your mother saved you, Nick. No child is born rotten. No matter what they say. We all come into this world the same. Cold and hungry, seeking warmth and comfort. Every last one of us. We're snatched out into this madness, dazed and confused and all we want is for someone to hold us and tell us that it's going to be okay. A steady hand to keep us from falling. You were lucky that you found one that held you instead of slapping you at every turn."

Nick scowled at his father as he realized for the first time the difference between them. While his mother had wrapped him up in her love and held him close to protect him from the world, his father had been shunned and left to fend for himself. With no mother to care what happened to him. Nobody had ever protected Adarian.

Not once.

Rather they'd all taken turns abusing and using him until he'd become the very monster he'd been foretold by destiny.

"I'm sorry."

He growled at Nick. "I don't want your pity, boy."

"That's not what I'm giving you, old man." Nick swallowed hard as the full tragedy of his father's life hit him square in the chest. Adarian couldn't even recognize what it was he was offering him. He had absolutely no concept of it. Couldn't even recognize what was right in front of his face.

And that burned Nick most.

"In spite of it all ... in spite of *you,* you worthless piece of dung, I do love you, Dad. I just wanted you to know it. You weren't much. But you were my father. The only one I'll ever have." And before he could stop himself, he hugged him.

At first, he thought Adarian was going to throw him against something. But instead, he fisted his hand in Nick's hair and held him tight to his chest. "You ever tell anyone about this and I'll rip out your throat."

Nick laughed at a very typical Adarian reaction. "Don't worry. No one would believe it, anyway."

Not even Nick really believed it. Maybe all of this was some hallucination. Maybe he was dead already. That would explain it.

But even so, he savored this one rare instance of being held by the man who'd fathered him. Even if he wasn't really a man.

You can't choose your father. You can only choose how you deal with him.

Nick was at peace with Adarian for the first time

in his life. He finally understood his mother's way of thinking and how it was that she managed to live the way she did. No wonder her soul was so beautiful.

If only his was.

But then that, too, was a choice.

Try as he might, he still wasn't a creature of forgiveness. He had a monster to stop. One who was determined to ruin him.

One who was out there, right now. Plotting against him and his friends and family.

"How do I get out of this book?"

"How did you get into it?"

Nick snorted. "Like I know? It's why I asked you here. I was hoping for some insight."

"Then you'd best be figuring it out."

"Well you're just all kinds of unhelpful, aren't you?" Nick rolled his eyes as he did his best to think of something, anything.

Sadly, nothing came to mind. How could this be?

He needed real help and he had no idea where his

help was. Or how to find it. He was about as lost as he'd ever been in his life.

"Where is Nick?" Caleb turned toward Kody.

"I don't know. He was supposed to be at the station with his mother. She said he left to go do homework and no one's seen him since."

"I've got a bad feeling about this." Aeron glanced up at the darkening sky over their heads. While storm clouds in New Orleans were nothing new, there was something ominous with these. Low hanging and jet black, they seemed a bit denser and more threatening than normal.

Not quite a natural phenomenon.

Kody nodded. "I hear you. Especially since I know Nick didn't have homework and he doesn't normally do any without a great deal of protesting."

"And whining," Caleb added. "Let's not forget the painful whining."

Kody scowled as a deep rumble sounded. "What exactly does a Sephirii army look like when it attacks?"

A tic started in Caleb's handsome cheek. "Honestly? A lot like *that*." He jerked his chin toward the storm clouds as he subconsciously rubbed his stomach where he'd been wounded earlier. "Aeron?"

"I see it, demon. Me hackles are up. Vawn!" he shouted. "Kaziel!"

Instantly, his companions materialized by his side, and took up defensive positions as they knew that whenever he called for them in such a manner it usually meant that danger was approaching. Fast. And their appearance like that probably wasn't the best thing for an afternoon in a crowded tourist town. But they were lucky enough that no one was paying attention to them. Rather they were all focused on the crackling electricity in the air, and seeking shelter from a storm that sounded deadly.

Threatening.

In human form, Kaziel dwarfed Kody. His long, pale blond hair framed a beautiful face that was marked with Celtic symbols for protection. Trained by the lady Shadow herself, the goddess Scáthach, he was the fiercest of the battle cŵns ever unleashed in war. And his pale green eyes showed the depth of his skills, and the tragedy that had been his harsh, tragic life.

As part of the infamous Arswyd Gan Drindod—the Terror by a Trinity—that consisted of him, Aeron and Vawn, Kaziel was legendary in Celtic lore.

Likewise, Vawn was ever as ready and eager to battle. But then the Rhyvawn Ddu—dark passionate one—was known for his love of all things deadly. Hence his current curse that had resulted in him being cast into the body of a woman. Because of his unrequited love for her, the sorceress had killed herself, and with her dying breath, had made it so that Vawn would be forced to spend eternity in her body, lamenting the fact that he'd never once paid attention to her. Now, he was forced to walk the earth as a female wraith who warned those about to die of their coming doom.

Tall and thin, with stringy red hair and dark eyes and lips, he was pretty enough as a woman—which irritated him to no end as men constantly came on to him, and he had no interest whatsoever in male attention.

And while Kaziel had an open sun tattooed on his forehead that aligned him to the light Celtic powers, Vawn held the tattoo of a black elongated star between his eyes that marked him firmly as belonging to the darker fey side. Indeed, the sorcerer preferred to play with the deadliest of magick, and had been known in his day to delve into things best left undisturbed. Things such as necromancy and death magick.

Aeron swore loyalty to both sides, and neither. It was what had made the three of them virtually invincible in their time. An unstoppable army of three no one had wanted to face in war.

Kody was glad to have them on her team. Even though they were weakened by curses and binding spells. They were still formidable.

And terrifying.

That lethal combination and their ability to remain calm and amused no matter the threat reminded her of her brothers. It also made her homesick at times.

"So . . ." Kaziel passed an irritated smirk toward Caleb. "Who's taking odds on Shadow not finding them swords anytime soon?"

Caleb scoffed. "Oh I'm taking odds on them being found. In my back or gullet, again. Possibly my head. Or another extremely uncomfortable body part. At the worst possible time."

Aeron snorted. "Have to say I'm in agreement with that, knowing our luck as I do."

"Aye, to that." Vawn was braiding his hair so as to keep it from his eyes. Or her eyes, rather. It was ever confusing as to how to refer to him as Kody was never quite sure, given his situation. Luckily, he was forgiving when it came to his gender, and only took offense whenever someone intended to offend him about it.

And for the first time, Kody considered how long the three of them had known each other and battled together. Nigh on an eternity. Brothers-in-arms. They would die before they failed each other. Die rather than betray. And bleed for each other without hesitation or faltering.

Everyone should have a friend like that.

It was a sad testament to the world that there were so few who did. Especially given the fact that they'd come together through adversity and from vastly different backgrounds. Indeed, Vawn, Aeron and Kaziel should be mortal enemies. Instead, they were bonded tighter than most families.

Vawn paused to scowl at her. "You all right, there, lass?"

Kody smiled. "Fine. At least as much as I can be given the unrivaled beauty of this particular day." Her tone dripped with her intended sarcasm.

"Truth to that. Me gaping wound be throbbing already. Can't wait for the next one to joining it."

Kaziel snorted as he moved to stand nearer to Vawn. "No worries, mate. I'll be tearing the throat of the next one what comes at you."

Caleb's gaze darkened. "We need to find our Malachai. I'm thinking this portends something foul."

Aeron cast a droll stare toward Caleb. "What are you? Mad, demon? I'm thinking this portends something ate our Malachai. Why else would he be missing?"

Kaziel nodded. "Agreed. He be in the belly of some beast most foul."

As much as Kody hated to admit it, they might be right. Because deep inside, she couldn't feel Nick, either. "Caleb? Can you contact him?"

The expression on his face confirmed her bitterest fears. "He's not on this plane, is he?"

Caleb swallowed hard. "No. May the gods help us. I think Noir has him."

And if he did . . .

This world was doomed.

CHAPTER 9

Closing his eyes, Nick felt himself falling through the aether. He was so lost to the grimoire now. To the power of it, and to his past and future.

All at once in his mind, he saw the lives of every Malachai. It filled him with so much anger and hatred that it was explosive. And at the same time, it saddened him that this was what his lineage had been left with.

Why?

Because of a war they hadn't started? Because two people had loved each other and it had angered others? How could so much tragedy come from something so simple and basic? Something so innocent and good? It staggered his mind.

Monakribos's father, Kissare, had been a Sephiroth of unquestionable loyalty and supreme power. The kyri of the Mimoroux—their top leader before Myone. He, alone, had given a heart to the darkest of all the gods, and taught her to love and care for something other than herself.

Just as Myone had done for Xev. No wonder the two of them had been so scared and paranoid. They had already seen how this played out. If the Source powers had been so cruel to their own over it, then they had held no hope for themselves.

Nick couldn't blame his great-grandparents at all.

Before time began, Kissare had been so pure of heart that he'd been chosen by the sword-spirit Takara as the first of the Sephirii to wield her in battle.

And, after Kissare's unjust death the gods had

demanded because he'd dared to fall in love with the goddess Braith, who had outed their relationship when she'd birthed their son Monakribos, Takara had refused to serve another warrior. The sword had taken a stand for the couple and the injustice done to them.

For centuries the sword had lain dormant, willfully silent, refusing all the Sephirii who attempted to activate and use her.

Until Jared.

Nick's maternal grandfather. How ironic, really. It made him wonder if Takara had known that Jared would be the last Sephiroth whose life would be bound to the final Malachai. That the sword had chosen her war partner intentionally with full knowledge that Jared would be used in the future for such a nefarious scheme by the very gods who'd first cursed Nick's lineage.

As it begins, so it ends.

Everything seemed to move in such cycles.

In his mind, Nick heard Jared's anguished shout in the past as Takara had been ripped from his hand and he'd been punished for trying to spare Jaden from his siblings. Heard Takara's own cries of misery when she'd been forcibly pried from his grasp. Whenever a Sephiroth bonded with his or her sword, their partnership was indivisible and eternal. To lose one was like having a limb ripped from the body.

Like Xev's wings being cut from his back . . .

Nick choked in sympathetic pain for them both. Even though they were technically enemies, they were also family.

We are destruction. That is our birthright.

Nick drew up short at the feminine voice in his ear. "Who are you?"

Out of the aether of the grimoire, appeared a haunting face. Paler than frost, with eyes of mercury, she reminded him of Acheron and Styxx. Ethereally beautiful, she was fragile in her grace and yet there was a power to her that charged the air around him. It ran through his body, causing every molecule of his being to stand up and take note of it.

Without being told, he knew this was Braith. Renamed Apollymi by Kissare, who refused to call her something that symbolized the shrieking, cold wind that had birthed her when Chaos and Order had first spun together to create her. The Sephiroth had come up with a name that meant the warmth and beauty she signified for him. He would never see her as anything else.

Not even when they'd tortured him for his love of her.

"So you're Acheron's mother." The words were out before Nick could stop them.

Her swirling silver eyes turned red as her white blond hair flared out as if she'd attack.

Nick braced himself.

But something calmed her down. "You're the friend of my Apostolos ..."

That was the name she'd given Acheron on his birth. "I am."

Her gaze softened. "And you're of my bloodline. Distantly. He must have sensed that in you." She walked a small circle around Nick. "It's probably why he trusted you when it's not in his nature to do so."

That was Nick's take on it, anyway.

Yet as she continued to walk her circle around him, a peculiar sensation went through Nick. One that was unmistakable and draining.

"You're not Apollymi!" He backed away from the fake goddess. "Who are you?"

Laughter echoed around him. It sent chills over his body. Hallucinating was one thing, but why this?

Why *her*?

"You know why."

He turned to find the other Malachai behind him.

"I'm not going to let you destroy everything! You know that. It's not in me."

Cyprian laughed. "You can't stop it. It's already happened. There's nothing you can do. I've already gotten away with it."

"Then why are you here?" Nick smirked, wishing he felt as cocky as he pretended to be. "You think I don't know the fear I see in your eyes? Yeah, I see your fear . . . *boy*. I can smell it!"

Not exactly true. But bluster seemed like a good move right now.

Yeah, that was usually a safe go-to when dealing

with anyone other than teachers, his mother, Caleb, Kody or Bubba. They would normally kick his butt for copping this attitude.

Others, however, were normally confused by it.

Or, in the case of Cyprian, taken down a peg. Because they weren't sure if Nick was bluffing or not. This was the only "lie" he was capable of pulling off with a straight face. Anything else and he was screwed.

For some reason, this one he could do.

Strutting, he moved closer in to eyeball Cyprian. "What's the matter, demon-boy? Can't find your tongue or your backbone?"

That went a little too far as it caused the fire to return to his eyes.

He reached for Nick and grabbed him by his ugly Hawaiian shirt. "I fear nothing!"

Yeah, they were related. Definitely. Nick needed to remember that, as being called out for cowardice was his bitch-switch too and it never failed to make him extremely suicidal.

Apparently, that little acorn had fallen straight

from the limb, hit the ground and dug its nubby little thorn in deep to the soil so as not to budge from its parent tree at all.

Consider him woked and learned on that one.

However, it also gave Nick a little more insight than ole Cyprian meant for him to have. "You fear the future as much as I do. Why else would you be here? Huh? What happens that it drives you back to babysit dear old dad? Who broke what?" He arched a goading brow at the demon. "C'mon, be honest. Bubba or Mark? You weren't dumb enough to leave *them* unsupervised with something important, were you?"

"They're both dead, you fool!"

Nick took that news like a sucker-punch. He literally felt it knock all the wind from his chest. "What?"

"It's true. They both go down, protecting *you*. Did you miss that memo, old man?"

Yeah, he had. But as soon as Cyprian spoke, he saw their deaths so clearly.

Worse, he saw his mother's grief. Heard her screams as she learned about Bubba, and took the news the same way she'd taken it when her sister had died.

Hard and personal. It all but destroyed her. And that was the one thing Nick could never stand.

Seeing his mom in any kind of pain.

Roaring, Nick grabbed Cyprian and shoved him back. "What did I do to make you hate me so much?"

"You had everything I wanted!" he growled. "They all loved you and I had nothing! *Nothing*! They couldn't even look at me without disgust and hatred!"

Nick was as shocked by those unexpected words as Cyprian appeared to be. Stunned, he stared into the demon's face that bore no semblance to his. 'Course a lot of that had to do with the fact that he didn't appear human at the moment, either.

Even so, his red eyes were filled with anguish. "I hate you for you're all that I never was, and will never be!"

Nick winced at the sincerity of those words, wishing he could fix this. While he now knew how Cyprian came into being, there was still one important piece he didn't have.

One piece he needed to fix this.

"Who's your mother?"

Cyprian laughed in his face. "You'll find out."

"Then it's not Kody?" It was a stupid question, given what he'd seen about the future. He knew it couldn't be her. But he had to have some confirmation to go on right now.

And anything, even something ridiculous, was better than nothing.

Hissing, Cyprian went for Nick's throat.

Nick barely got out of the way. "Yo, psycho-nut! Stop and talk! Why you got to be so violent?"

Aside from the obvious reason that he was a Malachai and it was their nature . . .

When Cyprian went to punch him, Nick ducked and caught him with a blow that caused him to stagger back. He then kicked him, twisted, and went to grab him.

In an impressive move, Cyprian swept to the side and came up behind Nick to wrap his arms around his chest. He held him incapacitated. "Have you any idea how hard it is for me not to rip open your throat and bleed you out at my feet?"

"Dude! You need some serious counseling and

professional help. And anger-management. At least let me lick your seatbelts and date your sister before you harbor this much animosity for me. Sheez! What'd I do, use all your data plan? Spike your kid's bottle with some Red Bull and give him ring pops for your favorite white sofa? Back over your petunias and not leave a note?"

Cyprian moved to make good on his threat to kill Nick.

The instant he did, Grim appeared and grabbed his hand to stop it from happening. His face was twisted into a grimace of fury as he backhanded Cyprian with enough force to knock him several feet away.

Stunned into a practical coma, Nick didn't move. He wasn't sure what part he reacted to most. That Grim was here. That he dared to attack another Malachai.

Or that he was defending him. 'Cause the last time they'd been together, Grim had threatened to see Nick in his grave and to dance and whizz on it.

All while laughing and stabbing at him.

Yeah, this made the least amount of sense out of all this insane madness.

Grim glared at Cyprian. "Kill him now, fool, and you'll end your own existence!"

Cyprian wiped at the blood on his lips. His breathing ragged, he glared at them both with an insanity that said he really didn't care.

It was almost enough to put some fear in Nick's spine. But his Cajun grit caught it before it could take root and sent it back down to the bowels of his mind so that it couldn't interfere with his better sense. As if anything could ever give him some common sense.

And true to form, Nick jutted his chin to goad Cyprian and Grim both. "C'mon, boy. Come get some." He let his wings out and his own Malachai form take over. Though to be honest, he had a bad feeling he was looking a bit wilted, and not up to his usual fearsome self.

Grim scoffed at his bravado.

Not exactly the reaction Nick was going for. It

actually kind of stung his ego and hurt his feelings. And it made him eternally glad that Kody wasn't here to see it. Doubly glad that neither Caleb nor Aeron witnessed the humiliation. Hard enough to look tough without his boys witnessing him getting dissed by the designer douche in bad clothes and knock-off Halloween gear.

But he couldn't help that.

And none of it was enough to make him back down.

Throwing his hand out, Grim used his powers to pin Nick to the wall behind him. "You need to return to being the useless snot-nose, smart-mouth guttersnipe who was hustling tourists and hanging out with your loser friends after school. Now be a good boy and drink your water!"

Shaking his head at Grim, Nick tried his best to push against him with his own powers. He cursed silently as they continued to fail him. "Ah, Grimmy, baby, why would I start pleasing you now, when we both know nothing makes me happier than to give you IBS?"

"Let's just cage him." Cyprian flapped his own wings.

"He has things he has to do for the future to play out the way we need it to."

"Then let me take his place. I know what needs to be done to set the future straight."

Nick went cold.

Grim started to curl his lip then paused. He slowly arched a brow as if he were actually considering it.

Nick began to panic at the thought. Surely they couldn't do that and get away with it. No one would fall for such a trick. Anyone could see through a fake copy. No one could be so stupid! "Ah bullcrap! That loser can't pull it off. Ain't nobody me, but me. My mama would know in an instant if he walked near her!"

And still Grim stroked his chin. "You know . . . you might be on to the solution, finally. You pulled it off once. Why not? Not even Acheron could tell you apart. Or Neria."

Cyprian sneered at Nick. "Who says we need him

here at all in the book? Lock him up. Feed him to the demons and weaken Noir even more."

"A twofer. I like that even more." Grim nodded. "All right. Let's do it."

Nick opened his mouth to protest.

But it was too late. They already had him caged.

CHAPTER 10

"Hi, Miss Kody. It's so good to see you! You're always so pretty and posh. Like a little angel from heaven. So how are you tonight?"

Kody smiled at the beautiful waitress as she came over to her table and set a glass of water down in front of her. "Fine, Mrs. Gautier. I'm supposed to meet Nick and do some homework. Is he in back, playing pool with Wren again? Or did Remi chase him upstairs to hide out with Alex?"

Barely past thirty, Nick's mom was a tiny woman. Dressed in the black Sanctuary staff t-shirt and jeans, she had her long blond hair pulled back into a ponytail. Frowning, she glanced around the sparse Tuesday evening crowd. "Actually, he's not here, sug." She pulled her phone from her apron pocket to check for messages. "He hasn't called either, which isn't like him. What time did he say he'd be here?"

"Seven."

Cherise screwed her face up. "It's not like him to be late. Never mind a whole fifteen minutes. Especially not with you. Weird. And I know he's not over at Michael's tonight. Him and Mark are gearing up for another go at their zombie survival apocalypse stew, and Nick's terrified they'll make him taste it for them. He should have gotten off work two hours ago—Kyrian normally calls me if Nick's ever held up for any reason. So I know he didn't run my boy late." She dialed the phone and held it up to her ear.

Kody didn't say anything as she checked her own

phone. There were no missed calls or messages from him.

Yeah, definitely not like her Cajun OCD Malachai who was maniacal about checking in with them.

"Hey, Boo. Where are you?" Cherise listened for a few minutes. "Yeah, well, Kody's here at Sanctuary. Said you're supposed to be meeting her?" She listened again before she finally sighed. "Okay. I'll tell her, but you need to make sure you stay on top of your promises. I raised you better than that, Nick. You don't keep a lady waiting. That's all kinds of wrong and you know it. You tell someone you're going to meet them, you're there on time. You hear me . . . ? All right. Love you, Boo. See you later."

Hanging up, she slid the phone in her pocket and offered Kody a sympathetic scowl. "I'm so sorry, Kody. Nick's off with Madaug. Said he forgot all about it. I don't know what's gotten into that boy lately."

Kody screwed her face up as she considered it herself. "He has been a little distracted the last couple of days."

Cherise's frown deepened. "Are you two crossed up?"

"No, ma'am." They hadn't even so much as passed an irritable snark at each other.

"Is he having trouble at school?"

No more than his normal run-ins with Stone and Mason. But everyone had trouble getting along with them. Even they got crossed up with themselves at times. "Not really."

"Fighting with Caleb, then?"

Kody shook her head. No one fought with Caleb as he tended to disembowel whatever annoyed him.

"Well, I can't figure it. But something's been weird. I know my boy and he ain't been the same since they questioned him about his friends." She swallowed hard. "Maybe that's it. Maybe their deaths hit him harder than I thought. I wonder if he needs to speak to someone about it?"

Yeah, that wouldn't go over well. Nick wasn't into sharing his more tender emotions with his closest friends, never mind a stranger. She'd never seen anyone more nimble at dodging questions . . . except

Caleb and Acheron. Only they could make Nick look like an open book. "I don't really think that's it, either, Mrs. Gautier. Pretty sure Nick would run for a door if you tried."

"I guess," she whispered under her breath. "It's like he's somebody else. Some days, I swear I feel like there's a stranger living in my little Nicky's body. Like a pod-person took him over and is staring at me as if he's never seen me before. I caught him the other day, at the door, with the weirdest look on his face . . . like he couldn't remember where his room was. Must be a teen boy, puberty-thing. He even forgot the words to his prayers at Mass. I can't remember the last time he did that." She patted Kody on the back and smiled. "Oh well. Let's not dwell on bad things. You sit right there and I'll bring you some of Mama Lo's famous bread pudding and an Oreo shake. That'll put a smile on your face and a hug in your belly."

Kody smiled at Cherise as she hurried off toward the kitchen.

And as she saw her disappearing through the door,

a memory hit her hard. One that had been buried way deep inside her . . . or rather a memory someone had restricted from her so much that she'd all but forgotten it.

Yet now with a burning clarity, she saw this restaurant and bar, not as it was today, but centuries in the future. Very similar and yet *very* different.

For one thing, Nicolette Peltier no longer owned it.

Her daughter Aimee did. Along with a Were-Hunter wolf named Fang Kattalakis who'd married Aimee after he and his brothers had moved their wolf pack to New Orleans.

At the same time Valerius Magnus had been assigned to town as a Dark-Hunter . . .

Dazed, Kody glanced around as her vision went in and out of the present and future. She saw the Were-Hunters who were currently in the crowded bar . . . The Howlers—the house band, only they were a bit older. The Peltier bear family who owned it now and who sat on the Omegrion Council that ruled over Werekind, only they had merged with other fey and preternatural creatures, to make a new family and home.

Dev, the huge muscled bouncer at the door would one day marry a Dark-Huntress named Sam—an Amazon warrior.

Max, the quiet dragon who lived in the attic upstairs, would be joined by his dragonswan and their children ... His brothers would leave Morgen's fey Circle where they currently resided behind the Veil and move in here, as well.

So *many* changes to come.

It staggered her mind. The former pirate, Rafael Santiago, would spend time here ...

Simon and Kassim. Even the Dark-Hunter Kit would become friends with the quiet Were-Hunter tiger named Wren, and both would fight to save the Devereaux sisters from the demons out to slay them.

And not all that far in the future. It would all start when Julian and Grace reunited with Kyrian.

They would all play a part in changing Nick's life and setting her own destiny in motion.

Time swam before her eyes, coalescing into one

moment. Nick holding their infant daughter in his arms, sitting only a few feet from where she currently was.

The dimpled smile on his face stole her breath as he fed her a french fry from his plate. "I wish my mother was here to see our little girl. She'd spoil her rotten."

Tears filled Kody's eyes as she saw herself dabbing at the drool on her daughter's chin. "I wish I could have met Cherise. I feel like I already know her."

"She was an incredible woman . . . like you." Joining them at the table, Acheron paused by Nick's side to make faces at their daughter. "And how's my little angel, huh?" he asked in a falsetto. "You keeping daddy up at night? I hope so! Make his ears bleed for me!"

Charity squealed in delighted laughter as if she understood him. Cooing, she reached for Acheron who took her in his arms and held her against his shoulder so that she could fist her hands in his long black hair.

"So where's Aunt Tory?" Kody looked around for his wife.

"Shopping with your mother for the baby," he continued to speak in that high-pitched tone that kept Charity laughing while he dodged her attempts to tug at his nose ring.

Kody smiled at the sight of his obvious care and tenderness. "She loves her uncle Ash."

"Like her mama did at the same age." Acheron kissed Charity's cheek.

"Yeah." Kody's father sighed as he came to lean over the back of Nick's seat. "There were times when I thought my baby girl preferred you to me, brother. Made me jealous until it dawned on me that it wasn't so much that, as she couldn't tell us apart." He winked at Kody who laughed at her father's tsking tone.

"Now, Daddy, that's not true. I always knew you two apart." Aside from the fact that her father kept his shorter hair their natural blond shade while her uncle dyed his black, the twins had different eye colors. Acheron's were swirling silver and her father's were blue. But other than that, there were identical copies of each other.

Except for one thing.

"And how is that?" Her father challenged.

She could tell by the suspicious light in his celestial eyes that he expected her to say the scars on his body, which was true, but like her mother, she didn't really see those. Rather it was a much more obvious difference. One that made her lean forward to whisper loudly above the club's din. "Your pockets don't bulge from carrying Simi's barbecue sauce and snacks."

Nick laughed. "That is true enough. Gah, I'll never forget that Thanksgiving when we almost ran out. You've never seen anyone run faster to make groceries, *cher*, than me in your life. I don't know who went paler, faster. Me or Ash."

"Oh that was definitely Alexion," Ash said with a laugh. "He was the most frightened by Simi's pout that day. I assure you."

"Nah, it was Savitar."

Kody tsked as she saw Simi approaching with her

husband. "Are you hearing the lies they're telling about you, Aunt Simi? Terrible, terrible lies!"

"Hey, Kody!"

Blinking, Kody left her memory to return to the present or the past . . .

For the first time, it was strangely confusing for her. As she finally had real memories of her life with Nick.

Takeshi had been right.

She'd been a lot older than Sroasha had led her to believe. Had led her to remember. She hadn't been the young teen she'd originally thought. They'd taken more than just her life from her.

They'd taken everything.

I was lied to . . .

Kody cursed as she realized what they'd done. They'd stolen the water of the Lethe. It was the only thing that explained all this. Hades gave it to all the dead so that they would have no memory of their life.

"How could I have been so stupid?" she breathed.

No, not stupid.

Trusting.

She'd believed in them and they'd intentionally misled her. Told her partial truths, and never given her enough of the past to refute it. It was easy to believe a lie when you only had one side of an argument. When you only had a bit of the facts. Too easy to paint someone as a scoundrel or villain. But she should have trusted her gut more.

Past behaviors were far better indicators of someone's habits. *A leopard doesn't change its spots.* She knew that adage well. Nick had never given her a reason to doubt his integrity. It was why she'd hesitated from the moment she met him. He'd never been anything other than a gentleman.

He lived his life with honor and code. Through and through. Unlike others, he wasn't a liar or a cheat.

Deep down, she'd known where the truth was.

Just as she knew right now that something else wasn't right. Cherise knew it, too.

All of this was wrong.

Nick wouldn't stand her up. Not like this and not once they'd made plans. It wasn't in him to be so thoughtless or selfish. Something else was going on.

Trust in what you know.

Nick wasn't a scoundrel or a liar. He didn't treat people like this. She had no reason to doubt him.

But the others . . .

She needed to find Caleb and Xev, and investigate what was really going on here. Nick was in trouble. Every part of her instinct told her that if they didn't sort this out, it would be too late.

He'd be lost to them forever.

CHAPTER 11

A lone and abandoned, Nick wandered helplessly through the barren fields of the Broken Mind. Everything here was twisted and dark. Shadows lurked and attacked. All around. All the time. Out of the countless scary places he'd been and hundreds of enemies he'd faced, this was by far the worst.

The most insidious.

Because he never saw the attacks coming. They were random and violent. Every time he dropped his guard, something swooped in, out of nowhere to bring him low.

As he staggered through the dark, the shrieking winds were deafening and he felt so alone and isolated. He didn't know how long he'd been here. It seemed as if eternity had passed as he fought to survive.

Cyprian had been right. No one knew the difference between the two of them. His son had taken his place and no one was the wiser. They really didn't know the shadow from the truth.

I'm completely forgotten.

He didn't matter to anyone. Not to his mom.

Not to Kody.

No one.

How could anyone be so deliberately blind? Did they want to be lied to? Or did they just not care?

I should just lie down and die. Really, why was he bothering? What did it matter at this point? He was so tired of the fight.

So tired of living.

I'm just a kid. If it sucks this bad at this age, why

should I bother trying to make it to adulthood? It'll only get worse.

He knew that for a fact. Wasn't like he hadn't seen the future and the mad nightmare that was waiting to swallow him whole.

Just like the beast rushing now to attack from the dark.

Shouting out, Nick swung at the hideous mass of a corpulent monster closest to him that was going for his throat. Its claws slashed as it tried to open his jugular and drain him dry. He had no idea why he didn't let the creature have him.

Maybe it was sheer stubbornness at this point.

Face it, his son sucked. His daughter, not so much. But Cyprian was a major douche nozzle. World would be so much better off without them both.

Yeah . . . he should do everyone a favor and just end this. Right here. Right now.

Throw his sword down and let these things eat him whole.

He almost succumbed to the weary desolation.

Why not? His mom was still young enough, she

could pick up the pieces. Have another kid. One who wouldn't get her killed in a few years.

Her and Bubba could make a nice life together, without him. Surely, he owed her that much.

His breathing ragged, he watched as the shadows shrank away as if they knew something inside him had changed. As if they sensed it, and were terrified by it.

"If you die, Nick, Acheron's wife will, too. And his sons won't be born. He'll never find it in him to make peace with Styxx, and Kody won't be born, at all. Neither will her brother, Ari. Urian will never know who his real parents are. Bethany will never be freed from her prison. For all the bad you think you'll do, you do a whole lot more good for the room."

Nick froze at the familiar lilting voice that rumbled through the darkness. "What?"

Vawn stepped forward so that he could see him more clearly. "It's true, mate. More than that, Kyrian'll die. You're the one who saves his life from Desiderius. Amanda won't find him without you. She won't have any idea where to look. And Valerius

Magnus's life. Without you, he'll never marry Tabby. You are crucial to them all. Even Talon and Zarek owe you. Dark-Hunters you have yet to meet. You're seeing only the bad right now, boyo. The pain. 'Tis easy to get lost to that pity. Believe me, I know."

He moved closer to Nick. "There's not a day what goes by I don't lament me life and what I've done in it. As the old song says, mistakes, I've made a few. But we do what we do, and we carry on as best we can. It's not how we deal with the best what life gives us that makes us who we are, Nick, it's how we pick ourselves up after we fall. It's not brave to stand tall underneath a shining sun, and with praise at your back. Bravery comes when there's no reason to get out of bed, and every reason to run for the door. But you make yourself crawl out and face the thundering hoard and hatred, knowing you're most likely going to get your arsling and pride hand-fed to you."

"Yeah, I've had enough of that. Thanks."

"We all have." Vawn gestured at his body. "You think I enjoy *this*?"

He had a point. Nick couldn't imagine anything much worse. That was his bitterest nightmare there. Waking up in someone else's body. Not knowing yourself when you looked in the mirror. He still hadn't gotten over the PTSD of it. It'd left a lingering impression on him and at least he'd been in an alternate Nick body, with some of the same things he knew.

Vawn's reality was a lot more crushing. He couldn't even begin to imagine *that* horror.

"But I don't have the luxury of death," Vawn continued. "This is me fate. Deserved or not. For all eternity and there's nothing I can do about it, except strap up and cope." He smirked. "Complain a bit, too, from time to time."

Nick snorted, knowing the truth was that Vawn seldom did that. Honestly, he almost never spoke about it at all. It was one of the things Nick admired most about him, or her, rather. The subject only came up whenever Vawn met someone like Aeron or Kaziel who knew him before his curse.

Otherwise, he soldiered on.

Reckless abandon. It was their unspoken code of honor. What kept them all going in the face of everything that sought to lay them low.

Which made Nick wonder something. "How are you here, Vawn?" Was he hallucinating from some kind of delirium?

He had to admit, that last round of demons had rung his bell pretty hard. Wasn't too far a reach to think he could be lying unconscious and dreaming all this.

Kaziel moved to stand by Vawn's side. "We're here to fetch you home, boyo."

In his demon form, Caleb swooped in to examine the monster Nick had last taken out. "Have to say, I'm impressed. Figured you'd be elbows deep in trauma. How'd you manage without us?"

Nick snorted at his droll tone. "You know me. God hates me too much to kill me and get this over with. Besides, give it a minute. Sure my friends will be back any second. You just missed them."

Caleb laughed. "That's a first."

"Right." Nick shrank his sword back to the size of

a pocket knife before he returned it to its flap. He drew up short as he caught sight of Kody.

Emotions tore through him so unexpectedly that for a minute, he couldn't breathe.

These were the times when he knew he loved her. When he finally understood how much Lil had meant to Caleb. Myone to Xev.

His mom to his dad.

That fist to the gut he got every time he saw her face. There was nothing else like it. She was the air he breathed. The sun that came after the torrential rain.

No, the rainbow.

His soul could be frozen and brittle, and a single smile from her face would warm every part of it. Set him on fire from the tip of his toes to the ends of his hair. He'd never known anything like it. No matter how bad he felt, the sound of her voice lifted him. The touch of her hand made his skin electric.

Unable to speak past the magnitude of everything rushing through him, all at once, he pulled her into his arms and crushed her against him.

And when she wrapped her arms around him and laid her head against his chest, he trembled.

Yeah, okay, this was why he fought. He remembered now.

For her.

She was so worth it.

"You okay, Boo?"

"Am now," he said gruffly. There was no need in letting her know how stupid he was being. How weak.

"Aww! You're so precious!" Kody's laughter turned cruel an instant before she changed into a hideous gigantic fanged, corpulent beast. The same beast he'd just killed.

Voracious in all things. It's unnaturally Titian hair reflected like gaudy rust in the dim shadows. Hissing, Nick stabbed it through the heart and drove his claws through the hollow of its jaw, catching the mandible. Fury caused his Malachai wings to launch through his back and it took control of him for the mockery. Before he could stop himself, he curled his fingers around the bone and wrenched the mandible free of the sinew and muscles.

It was disgusting! But he couldn't help it and it didn't satisfy his need for vengeance or his cry of indignation. He wanted more.

He wanted every last drop of its blood to coat his body and drink the beast dry. He was through playing these cruel games with them.

No more!

"Who's next!" he shouted to the twisted trees surrounding him. "Bring it on! I'm done with you all! You want some of me? You better come prepared!"

Forget the Malachai. Generations of Cajun blood boiled inside him. They were swamp people and they didn't take injustice and mockery lying down. They gave it back with both fists and two kicks.

He ran at the next shadow that came for him.

zura pulled back the second she saw the degree of fury inside the Malachai and the form he'd taken. No longer was his skin mottled red and black.

He was a pure saturated ebony. So dark that he

absorbed all light itself. Matte and resistant to all color. He took in the living essence of everything around him. It was something she hadn't seen since the beginning of time.

Something wholly unexpected.

Even her brother, Noir, the darkest of all the ancient gods hesitated in respectful trepidation. "Well, this is new."

"Indeed."

And by the expression on her brother's face, she could tell that this Malachai wasn't feeding his powers.

Another first.

"Are you all right?"

Noir's nostrils flared. "Do I look all right?"

Honestly? He looked a bit green. Which contrasted greatly with her naturally blue skin. Knowing better than to answer him when he was this upset, she quickly changed the subject. "This must be why Cyprian and Laguerre hid him from you."

"How can a Malachai drain me?"

Azura felt the blood leave her face as the only

possible answer came to her. It was the same reason they'd demanded the life of Braith's husband. Why they'd made sure that their sister never birthed another brat from Kissare. "He would have to be part Sephiroth."

And Noir had drank his blood . . .

That would not only weaken, it could kill him.

Shrieking, her brother recoiled as if he recognized the truth of her words, and was every bit as disgusted that someone else might have discovered their one weakness. "Get those swords! Rebuild our army and turn them to our side. We need them to bring down Cam and Verlyn! I want Rezar's throat!"

"That's all well and good, but we don't know where Rezar is."

He turned on her with fury in his black eyes. "A Sephiroth can find him! Don't be stupid!"

"I wasn't trying to be stupid." She ground her teeth at him. And if it was so easy for a Sephiroth to find him, he'd have been located. Sadly, there were only two people alive who could call Rezar out of hiding.

Braith, whom the god loved and would do

anything for. And Rezar's brat, Bethany. Too bad for them that Bethany was currently being held as a living statue, prisoner in a realm where neither of them could venture.

Yeah, neither option was open to them. It was so frustrating. He was right. She was stupid.

Yet not so stupid that as she turned back to her brother, she didn't realize something else.

The color of his skin.

Green.

Verlyn.

Suddenly, everything clicked into place as she remembered the end of the war. The fall of the Sephirii army. Verlyn had been charged with rounding up their swords and destroying them.

Behind their backs, the Kalosum had taken Seraph medallions and created a new army with a loophole. While not Sephirii, they were made up of their children.

The same concept, only instead of their swords holding the more powerful creatures who'd bonded with the Sephirii such as Takara, these swords held

Seraphim souls who would bond with their own kin during combat so that they could fight against her and Noir, and whatever forces they unleashed.

I should have known ...

They could never trust their siblings. For creatures who claimed to be goody two-shoes, they were ever plotting mayhem.

And this time, those jackals might have finally found the way to destroy them. Terrified, she pulled Noir close and took him home to their dark palace to hide before Jaden or anyone else learned their secret.

She would have to walk carefully and guard this, as it could undo them both. This was treacherous ground, indeed.

"What are you plotting?" Noir accused.

"Shh!" She laid him back in his bed. "You rest. I'm going to find a way to use those swords to make Tarhnen from them." The Tarhnen were the dark Sephirii who'd been corrupted. With them, they could turn the tables on their brethren and overthrow the balance.

Brushing Noir's dark hair back from his forehead,

she offered him a determined stare. "Have no worries. We will rise and they will regret this."

No one got the better of them. Not without paying
a bitter, harsh price. This war was far from over.

CHAPTER 12

N ick shook as he felt the powers of the Source flowing through him. It was the first time he'd ever tasted real blood. And what blood it was.

Colors exploded around him as every voice in the universe cried out at once. The sound hit him like a thrumming drumbeat that reverberated through his entire body until his own heart synched to it and they pounded as a single unity.

He felt the cosmic alliance. Was this what

Acheron lived with? If so, he couldn't imagine the responsibility the Atlantean lived with. It was heady and terrifying.

I could destroy the world . . .

He understood the power. It wouldn't be hard. As the Malachai, he had the ability to call forth every dark entity from its prison or corner and force it to his command.

No one born of the Mavromino could deny him.

Nothing can contain me.

Nick tilted his head as he realized a truth that had escaped even his father. Because his father had never dared what he'd just done. Lifting his hand, he threw a burst of fire through the membrane that held him inside his grimoire.

While a part of him doubted his discovery, another part knew the truth.

Lucky for him, that part wasn't insane. His fire caught and spread into a circle in the air, hovering like a manhole. It formed a sizzling ring of fire that made a portal from this world back into his own.

Like a dialing a phone. All at his command. Even
Grim would have been impressed that Nick had
finally learned to master the very powers they'd all
tried so hard to teach him.

I am the Malachai.

Unrestrained.

May the gods help them all now. Honestly, even
he was scared by it. *I have to remain in control of it.*

So long as he did, everything would be okay. He
couldn't let his emotions rule him. And whatever he
did, he had to keep reign on his temper.

Defy my destiny.

He should be good at that. He'd never been the
kind of kid to mind anyone or do what was expected
of him. If he was, he'd be in county lock-up now.
Not an honor student at one of the most exclusive
prep schools in New Orleans. A school that rarely
took in students who weren't from the blue-bloods
who'd founded it. Or the kids of Dark-Hunters, their
Squires or Were-Hunters.

Yet Nick had scored higher than anyone in the
school's history.

Yeah, if he could do that, he could do this.

With a deep breath, he flew through the portal, into his bedroom and quickly changed into his human body. Then, he waved his hand and closed the portal behind him, sealing it shut.

A nervous twinge made the hairs on the back of his neck rise. Could it really be this easy?

He still wasn't completely sold. After all, tricks on him were commonplace. Especially here lately. It would be routine for this to be yet another act of cruelty.

Cautiously, he made his way through his room, looking for any sign of another attack. Not to mention, the last thing he needed was for someone to see two Nicks. Life was confusing enough. And while he was creative, he doubted he could make anyone believe a "good twin" versus a "bad twin" scenario. Especially his mom, since she knew for a fact that he was an only child.

"Thought you were going out?"

Nick jumped at the unexpected deep voice. Cursing, he jerked around to face Zavid who was in human form. "What are you doing here? Besides trying to kill me? With a heart attack?"

Zavid normally stayed with Caleb.

Cocking his head, Zavid sniffed at the air then relaxed. "Oh thank the gods, it's *you*."

"Me?"

"Yeah. You. Not the fake Nick. I have to tell you, I've been getting sick as a dog of his crap."

If Nick wasn't still hyperventilating, that would be funny given that Zavid was a shapeshifting Hel hound.

Was he dreaming?

Nick wasn't sure if he could trust in this, or not. "You knew?"

"Of course I knew. Took a bit to make the others realize it. But he doesn't smell like you." Zavid pulled him back into his room.

Nick relaxed a degree. "Did anyone else notice?"

"Only your mom. Though she blamed it on a faze you were going through. And Kody, too, but it took her a little while."

That made him feel a lot better that he wasn't

completely irrelevant and replaceable. "How long have I been gone?"

"Two weeks."

"Two weeks!" Nick started to flip over it, until he remembered something. "Did the weasel pass my Chem test? Or do I have summer school?"

"He aced it."

For that, he could almost forgive Cyprian. "Good. 'Cause I'd have knifed him if he'd damaged my GPA."

"Seriously? That's your biggest concern, given everything else?"

"End of the world ... and a close second is being forced to attend junior college. Yeah! Have you seen the difference in the campuses?"

Suddenly, Zavid had that disgusted look Caleb got so often around him.

"Don't you even take that expression, old dog. It's a big deal. I'm supposed to go to Loyola and Tulane. Can't do that with failing grades." He gestured toward his desk where his phone was normally docked. "Check with Caleb. He'll tell you what my future was."

"Anyway," Zavid said, grabbing Nick by the arms. "Getting back on point. Your little friend has been playing havoc with everyone. It's so bad, Bubba's banned you from his store. He even threatened to shoot you if he saw you again."

Nick's jaw went slack. "Pardon?"

"Yeah. Your mom's about ready to call in a priest to have your exorcized."

"That's priceless. So what happens if you exorcize a Malachai?"

"You really don't want to find out."

"If it's done to Cyprian, I do."

Zavid rolled his eyes. "Fine. Get Caleb. He knows a few to call. I dare you."

Normally, Nick would call that bluff and raise it, but not today. He was a little tired of the fight. "So how do we get rid of this jackass?"

Before Zavid could respond, Nick felt a peculiar ache in his stomach. It was a soured feeling. Like being sucker-punched after eating way too much cake. For a moment, he feared he was going to be sick.

"Nick?"

He couldn't breathe. The worst premonition went through him. One he prayed he was wrong about.

Unable to stand it, he teleported to Kody's house.

The moment he appeared in her living room, he knew something was wrong. And it wasn't just because the place was wrecked. This was more than that.

Tears filled his eyes as he choked on her name. He couldn't bring himself to say her name. His fear was too profound for that. Because if she didn't answer . . .

Please, be here.

Be okay!

Nick ran through the rooms, looking for her. Each one showed the remains of a vicious fight. Pictures were torn from the wall and shattered on the ground. Furniture overturned and busted. But it was the blood on the walls and floor that made his wings shoot out.

And when he reached her bedroom, everything in his world shattered.

For a full minute, he couldn't breathe. He couldn't move. All he could do was stand there as he saw her lying on the bed. Dressed in her white Nekoda uniform, she was pale and unmoving. Her mother's bow was on the floor near her. As was her sword.

Over and over, Nick saw the future where she died.

He saw the day he met her. The way she'd defended him against Mason and Stone at school. Heard her laughter as she teased him.

Silent tears burned his cheeks as he stumbled toward her.

"K-k-kody?" But it was too late.

She was gone.

Throwing his head back, Nick roared as pain filled him and prayed for this to be another cruel trick. Prayed that he'd wake up in the grimoire.

"Nick?"

Hissing, he turned toward the sound of Caleb's voice to find his protector in the doorway, staring at him.

The expression on Caleb's face said that he wasn't sure it was Nick he was looking at. Or that he could trust his own eyes. "What happened?"

His breathing ragged, he glared at Caleb. "That's what I want to know! What happened, Caleb! Where were you!"

"Hunting for you."

"Why did you leave her unprotected?"

Caleb didn't answer.

Nick started to attack. The only thing that kept him from it was the last shred of sanity he had that recognized the agony inside Caleb's eyes. That haunted horror they shared. And the one worse bit that said he was reliving the moment when he lost his own wife.

Never had he seen Caleb appear weak or affected by anything.

Until now.

"I wouldn't have ..." Caleb's words broke off as his eyes teared up. His breathing turned every bit as ragged as Nick's as he staggered closer. "Can't you bring her back?"

"I don't have those powers. Do I?"

"No, you don't."

Nick gasped as he heard Kody's voice. Snapping around, he saw the shadowy outline of her winged Arel form.

She reached for him, then dropped her hand. "I'm sorry, Nick. I tried."

"I can't do this, Kody. Not without you."

Her lips trembled. "Of course you can, baby. You did it before."

"I didn't know you, then." But no sooner had those words left Nick's lips than he saw a peculiar flash. A glimmer of something that hadn't been there before.

Kody let out a bitter laugh as she nodded. "Yeah, Nick. It's what you're thinking. Crazy, huh?"

"No . . . it can't be."

She swallowed hard. "I have to go. But I couldn't leave without saying goodbye. I love you. Now and forever." She started to fade.

"Kody! Kody, wait!"

She hesitated.

"I will find a way back to you. You hear me? I swear to God."

"I'll be waiting." Her gaze went to Caleb. "Take care, my Boo. You'll need each other."

Then she was gone.

Unable to breathe or cope, Nick raked his hands through his hair. "Caleb . . . tell me what to do."

"You know I can't."

In that moment, he really did want to die. The last thing Nick wanted was to feel this much pain. Clenching his fists to his sides, he roared at the injustice of it all. It wasn't right.

It wasn't fair!

Since when is life fair?

Kyrian and Acheron would be the first to laugh in his face about that whine. Nothing about life was ever fair. He knew it as well as they did.

And he hated life for that fact. He always had.

Because it should be.

Maybe that was what adulthood really was, after all. The moment when you realized that the sheet wouldn't tally at the end of the day. That one column would always have more than the other. And no matter what you did or how hard you tried, you just couldn't get the columns to balance.

Victim or victor.

Did he really have a choice? Because right now, it sure didn't feel like it.

No. This was life ramming it down his throat and shoving it in a place where he didn't think the sun would ever shine again.

"I'm done, Caleb."

Caleb scowled at him. "What?"

"I mean it, this time. Why are we bothering? Why are you fighting, still?"

He grabbed Nick by the shirt and jerked him so close that their noses practically touched. His dark gaze scorched him with fury. "For the reason you're going to stop feeling sorry for yourself. Strap up and kick that bastard's ass. You made a promise and we don't break our words."

"We're demons."

"And we don't break our words. I made a vow to Lil. Just as Xev made one to Myone. And you just gave yours to Kody. We fight, not for ourselves, but for what we love." He shoved Nick back. "You asked me what you should do. That's it. You fight."

Wiping his eyes, Caleb sniffed. "Go on. See to your mom. I'll take care of Kody."

Nick hesitated. "Did you hear back from Shadow?"

"He hasn't found the swords."

"What's that mean?"

"That our enemies can rebuild their army."

Nick's stomach drew so tight that he felt sickened with those words. "That's how they get us in the future, isn't it?"

Caleb didn't say anything. He didn't have to. The expression on his face said it all.

"We can't win this, can we?"

"I don't know, Nick. The cost has been so high."

"But why? We're fighting for what's right. How can they just walk all over everything that's good and decent, and no one stops them? No one else seems to care about the evil they do. Why should we suffer for the rest?"

Caleb let out a bitter laugh. "You're asking me?

The daeve demon? Remember whose side I was on originally? It wasn't this one."

He had a point.

Clearing his throat, Nick wiped at his eyes. "I figured out my powers, Cay."

"About time."

Nick snorted. Yeah, it was. He looked back at Kody and choked on another wave of tears as he realized it was too late for her.

"Ambrose came back to the past and tried to stop it. Three times."

"I know." Caleb rose to his feet while Nick gently wrapped his jacket around Kody's body.

His heart splintering, Nick brushed his hand through Kody's hair. "I'm thinking that if this didn't work, we have one more option."

"Nick—"

"Hear me out, Caleb." Nick glanced past him to Zavid. "This is a longshot, but it's time for the Hail Mary pass. We couldn't stop them here and now. I'm thinking we stop Cyprian in his own time."

"How? You don't know when that is."

"No, but we know someone who does."

Caleb scoffed bitterly. "He won't let you do this."

"I think he will."

One way or another, Nick was going to force him to it.

CHAPTER 13

"You're out of your Cajun mind." Takeshi literally choked as soon as he heard Nick's idea.

Nick shook his head. "Kody's gone." He swallowed hard against the burning lump in his throat that mirrored the one in his stomach. His mood kept vacillating between nauseated grief, righteous fury, and hopeless defeat.

Honestly, he was beginning to think his emotions needed a traffic cop as they swung from one extreme to the other so fast that even he was having a hard time keeping up with them.

One word. One scent. It took next to nothing to send him careening over the edge to near breakdown levels.

And he knew if anyone understood that, it was the ancient being in front of him. "What would you do if you lost Nashira?"

The darkness in Takeshi's eyes churned like a storm front. It was palatable and terrifying. And enough to make Nick take a step back.

"Then you know how I feel right now."

Takeshi winced, rubbing his hand over his heart as if it ached from the mere thought of it. "I'm sorry, kid."

"And I'm mad as hell. I want blood for this and I will have it." More than that, he was heartbroken and wounded to the core of his soul. Really, there were no words to describe how screwed up he felt. Defeated and beaten, and yet the rage and need to strike back burned so deep inside him that it took everything he had not to lash out and annihilate the world, and everyone in it. The fury he felt that everyone around him was going on with their lives, unscathed and untouched, neither knowing nor caring that Kody was gone, while he felt like this . . .

It was all he could do to hold himself back. He wanted to see it all burn to the ground. Feel the cinders of souls rain down on his Malachai skin.

Only then would the fury in his blood be appeased.

This must have been how Kyrian felt when his soul screamed out for vengeance after his wife betrayed him, and Artemis came to make him a Dark-Hunter.

Nick finally got it with a clarity he wished to God he didn't know. He'd always wondered what could make someone sell their soul for vengeance.

Now he knew.

There were some questions you shouldn't ask, because you didn't want the answers to them. If the truth were known, he couldn't take it anymore. He was too young to be this tired.

Life had finally kicked him in the stones one time too many. He just didn't want to get up again. Every option seemed closed and alien. In some ways, it was like being inside someone else's skeleton. As if his own skin didn't fit anymore.

While he'd outgrown many shoes and clothes over his lifetime, this was the first time he'd felt as if he'd outgrown his own body. Must be how a snake felt right before it shed its skin . . .

"It makes perfect sense. I drink the water of the Lethe and forget this and everything that's happened since the night Kyrian saved me. Caleb can use his magick to bind my powers again and plug in the right memories. That way, my life will go on and reset the way it was supposed to be. I won't remember Kody or being the Malachai. Everything will be normal."

Takeshi rubbed at his chin. "What about your mom?"

"Taken care of. Caleb's going to help me with that, too. We'll find a way to stop it when I'm older and able to better handle this. I just need you to get me to the future, later on. Can you do it?"

Takeshi let out a deep breath. "I can do lots of things. But as Acheron says, just because you can doesn't mean you should. And what you're asking could get us both smacked down in ways you don't understand."

"I know. But I need you to do this for me ... Please. Help me save my mom and Kody."

Takeshi met Caleb's harsh stare. "And you're good with this, Malphas?"

Caleb let out a bitter laugh. "I don't know. It's Nick, so I'm sure it'll get screwed up in ways we can't even conceive. But he's right. I don't see any other way to get them out of here and control the disaster they're bringing down on us."

Nick handed Takeshi his grimoire. "In exchange for this favor, I'll leave you with permanent custody of Nashira. You two can be together forever. With my blessings."

He cursed under his breath. "My one weakness."

"And Kody's mine."

Taking the grimoire, Takeshi clutched it against his chest as a tic worked in his jaw. "You found the one bit of leverage you knew I could never say no to."

"Yeah, I know. I'm a Malachai. Fighting dirty is what we do best."

"And you're sure about this?"

He nodded. "It's the only way. I just need a few hours to clean this disaster up."

"All right. I'll see you at midnight."

Nick inclined his head to him. As he started past Caleb, his friend stopped him.

"It's been my pleasure, Malachai."

Those words actually made his throat even tighter as another wave of tears choked him. It took everything he had to hold them back because he knew Caleb didn't say things like that lightly. "That must have hurt to say out loud."

"Like the fires of hell scalding my tongue."

Nick laughed. "Thank you, Cay. For everything you've done. For every wound you've taken in my name." He held his hand up. "I wish I could always remember just what a great brother you've been."

Caleb took it and pulled him in for a bro-hug. "I can't believe I might actually miss you."

"Yeah, me and kudzu. We defy all logic, and tend to grow on the most unlikely of things."

Caleb clapped him on the back. "That you do."

Nick handed his phone over. "I put everything in there you'll need. Including the dates I know. Please, make sure nothing happens to Bubba and Mark."

"I will do my best. But you know how they are. Can't help what they get into when I'm not around and they're determined to play with explosives and buckshot."

Well, there was that.

"Take care." Tapping him on the shoulder, Nick used his powers to teleport home. He had one last bit of business that he needed to see to.

Track down Cyprian.

This wasn't going to be pretty. But if the truth were known, he was looking forward to it.

He'd barely reached his room before Xev was there, in human form.

"You're not really planning this level of stupidity, are you?"

Nick shrugged and flashed his famous Cajun grin. "Ah, now, *Grand-père, c'est moi.* Of course I am. *Laissez les bons temps rouler!*" Let the good times roll. "Man's gotta do what a man's gotta do." He sobered as he thought about what lay ahead for them. "I didn't start this dance. But last call's on me. Free drinks, all around."

Xev sighed. "I never understand ninety percent of anything you say."

"I know." Nick hugged his great-grandfather. "I'll miss you, Grans."

"I will not miss you calling me that." Xev tightened his arms around him and held him for a moment longer. "But I will miss you, too." He brushed his hand through Nick's hair. "Keep your nose clean."

"You, too. Don't kill Caleb."

"Make no promises."

Nick laughed as he started cleaning out his pockets to hand over all his Malachai items. They couldn't afford for him to remember anything. Not if his plan was to work.

And he prayed it would.

For Kody and his mom.

As soon as Xev had everything and was gone, Nick used his powers to locate the other him.

To his disgust, he realized Cyprian was at

Sanctuary where his mom was working. Of course he was. Freeloader.

Fake. Pretentious. Could never be himself. He had to be a second-rate copy.

It was disgusting, if the truth were known. *I would much rather be a first-rate copy of myself and fail, than be a second-rate copy of anyone else. For any reason.*

Furious, he headed straight over to the back alley that was only a couple of blocks from their condo. There wasn't anyone in Sanctuary's courtyard, or much of anything else for that matter. An old iron fountain and some greenery. The bears didn't come outside much. He wasn't sure why.

About the only one he ever found out here was Jose, their cook. Sometimes one of the human waitresses.

Intending to lure Cyprian outside, he headed for the door. But he only made it halfway there before Simi appeared by his side.

"You really going to forget us, Akri-Nicky?"

Her pout made his stomach tighten. He would

definitely miss the Charonte demon. She'd been a lot of fun to hang out with. "Just for a little while. We'll meet again when I'm older."

Simi pouted. "Well, poo, demon-boy. The Simi was very fond of her friend. I shall miss you!"

"I'll miss you most of all, Miss Simi." He kissed her cheek.

Instead of allowing him to pull away, Simi held him close. "Don't keep the sadness in your heart, demon-Nicky. It would make Akra-Kody very sad if she knew you hads it there."

"I know." Nick wiped at the sudden moisture in his eyes and he cleared his throat gruffly. "Can I ask a favor, Sim?"

"Surzies."

"Can you go get the fake Nick and get him out here for me?"

"Like I did lasterday?"

Nick laughed at the way she said yesterday. He would definitely miss the Simispeak. "I wasn't here lasterday."

"Oh yeah, that was the fake demon-boy. Okies,

I goes gets him for you! Wait right here and I'll be back licksy spilt!"

Still amused by her speech, Nick didn't move from the alley until Simi and Cyprian returned.

The humor died on Cyprian's face the instant he saw Nick waiting for him. His eyes turned a vibrant red. "What are you doing here?"

"What do you think?"

"You're wasting your time."

"Nah. Wasting yours." Without telegraphing his intentions, Nick punched him where he stood. "That's for Kody, you sorry piece of dung!" Then he hit him again and again, as he unleashed every ounce of his grief and agony on him.

His fists hurt and his knuckles throbbed as the skin over them started bleeding. Nick didn't care. Not now. Not when he wanted a pound of flesh from the one who'd hurt what he loved most.

Cyprian began to laugh. "You can't hurt me! The more you hit, the weaker you become." He spit blood in Nick's face.

His fatal mistake.

As Cyprian moved in to slug him, Nick ducked and came up with his Malachai dagger. He drove it straight into Cyprian's ribs as he stared in to a pair of eyes that were identical to his own.

With a stunned expression, Cyprian staggered back. "You ... you can't kill me! You're my father!"

Nick stabbed him again then used the dagger to drive him back into the wall so that he could hold him there with it. "Not yet I'm not. You're just another demon out to end me, and Nick Gautier don't go down for no demon. Or anybody else. They should have told you that." He felt his powers growing stronger as Cyprian's weakened. "You killed Ambrose, boy. You didn't kill Nick."

Oh yeah.

He had this ...

Nick was becoming the full Malachai again.

Cyprian laughed weakly. "You might have killed me, here and now, but this isn't over. All you've done is freed an even worse enemy. *Bon chance, mon père. Bon chance.*" And with that he slid slowly toward the ground.

Nick felt his jaw go slack as his mind whirled from the threat. A sudden light pierced the dim alley, almost blinding him an instant before it consumed his son's body.

Cyprian disintegrated in a matter of seconds. Nothing was left behind.

Not even a stain. There was no mark at all to say that Cyprian had ever existed.

Shaken with that knowledge, Nick wiped the blood off his dagger then handed it to Simi. "Please make sure Caleb gets that."

"Okies. But where you going?"

"To see my mom before I forget everything I know." And to make a few notes for Caleb. He wouldn't have long before the water took affect and left him completely ignorant.

He winked at her. "You take care, Simi."

And with that, he headed to the front of Sanctuary where Dev stood guard at the entrance.

"Hey, Squire squirt. Back so soon?"

Nick laughed nervously at his question. Dev must not have been able to see through Cyprian's trick.

"You know me. I'm like a piece of gum. Always attaching myself to your favorite pair of shoes ... usually when you're on a date and trying to look cool."

Dev shook his head as they shook hands, then Nick went inside.

Life was ever changing. Ever in motion.

Victim or victor.

No guarantees. Except one. The day you stopped trying, you were guaranteed a loss. So long as you were trying, you weren't defeated.

You were trying.

And Nick Gautier would never stop trying. Over, under, around or through. He would find a way to save his mom.

And keep his promise to Kody.

"I'll be back for you, Neria," he whispered under his breath as he saw his mom across the room, taking orders at a table. "And we're going to save Cyprian."

He had no idea how. But he wouldn't stop until he succeeded.

Or died trying.

CHAPTER 14

May 2000

Caleb let out a tired breath as he watched Nick running toward the school's entrance.

"Is he ever on time?"

Snorting at Xev's stupid question while they sat on a tree branch, he shook his raven's head. "You know better."

In the form of a large white house cat, Xev swished his tail. "Well, at least you finally got out of high school."

"You're not funny, brother."

They both went still as they picked up on the death shadow heading up the steps, in the same direction Nick had just vanished.

Disgusted, Caleb looked at his brother. "You were saying?"

"Go get 'em, tiger."

"What? You're not coming?"

"You got this. Besides, I'm going to check on Nick and make sure he's all right."

Grumbling, Caleb flew toward the entrance. Still invisible, he transformed into his demon's body and went inside so that he could protect his charge.

Xev reached up and touched Myone's winged necklace around his neck before he used his own powers to return to an invisible version of his demonic self. Even though Nick was now ignorant of their existence, they still had to watch his back.

All around them, evil flourished.

It was a thankless job they would carry out until Nick was older. Not that Xev minded.

For the first time in history, he was happy and content with his lot. While he might not have his wife or his son, he had Jared's daughter and grandchild near him.

His legacy.

And they were much better than a demon like him deserved.

Nick paused as he felt the wind near him shifting. "Kody?"

Brynna looked up from her lab worksheet to frown at him. "Pardon, Gautier? Have you lost your mind? Name is Addams? Hello? I know you know me. We've known each other for years."

Blinking, Nick shook his head. Where had that name come from? The only one he knew was the Were-Hunter, Françoise Peltier, at Sanctuary who went by Cody as a nickname. But he wasn't looking for a guy.

For some reason, he felt like it should be a girl's name.

How odd. But then, his entire purpose in life was to serve as an example to others on what they should never do.

And apparently, he'd eaten paint chips as a kid or something. 'Cause he must have brain damage to be spouting off like this.

Yet . . .

Here lately, it felt like something was missing from his life. Like something had been here once and it was now gone.

But he didn't know what.

Must be graduation jitters.

Yeah, he'd go with that. Though it wasn't like he didn't know what he'd be doing after graduation. Basically the same as now.

Squiring for Kyrian. Occasionally, running errands for Talon and Ash. Doing a few odd shifts for Bubba and Liza in their stores. And going to school.

Only instead of St. Richard's he'd be at either Loyola or Tulane. He just had to decide which one he wanted to attend since he'd been accepted into both.

"Are you listening, Mr. Gautier?"

Nick glanced up at his teacher. "Yes, ma'am. Always." After all, he had a bright future to look forward to, and he had no intention of screwing it up.

EPILOGUE

New Orleans, 3247

Ambrose scowled as he felt a strange presence in his study. It was intense and powerful. Unlike anything he'd felt in a long, long time.

Immediately on alert, he flashed himself into the room to confront who or whatever dared to defy his sigils and invade his domain. Whoever it was, they would regret this stupidity.

He'd make sure of it.

At least that was his thought until he came face-to-face with the last thing he expected.

A snot-nosed teen who bore a frightening resemblance to himself. Right down to a tacky Hawaiian shirt that all but glowed in the dark.

What the hell? He'd all but forgotten his mother's insistence on him wearing such travesty.

Stunned, he realized the kid wasn't alone. Caleb was with him. Along with Aeron, Kaziel and Vawn, and a teen girl he didn't recognize.

"What is this?"

The boy stepped forward. "You're going to want to sit down for this, demon man. After all, I got the idea from a future you. Brace yourself. I'm the old you from the past, and I'm here so that we can fix the timeline you screwed up. And save the life of our son." He glanced over his shoulder at the others. "Take my word for it. The end is just beginning."